PHOENIX RISING

a VS GRIFFIN novel

PHOENIX RISING

Printed in the United States of America

PGM, Inc LLC Publishing, 2020

ISBN 9780578460628

Connect with the author!

www.vsgriffin.com

PGM, Inc Publishing
www.pgmincllc.com

Dedication

This book would not exist without "The makings of me."

God the Father, Jesus the Son, and the Holy Spirit. I must thank my parents, my children, my family, and especially my best friend Biscuits and Gravy.

I am eternally grateful for the sacrifices you made and make for this to happen. I carry all of you in my heart, always.

Blessings... Love... Light

Prologue

"You have my sincerest condolences." It was a phrase that she remembered all too well. In the days, and months, after the tragic accident - it was all, she'd heard. Usually, whispered to her quietly before the speaker awkwardly pulled her in for an embrace. It wasn't their fault. They meant well, but few knew the right words for this type of situation. Your child is supposed to bury you, not the other way around. It was an experience that she wouldn't wish on even her worst enemy. After reading the card again she put it away, making a mental note to thank the sender for their condolences. She appreciated the sentiment, even though it did nothing to stop the pain. After the dead are buried, life continues to go on. A bitter pill that she was tired of swallowing, she was tired... so utterly tired. For the last week she'd spent her time inside of a bottle, using the dark liquid to take the edge off of the biting grief she'd slowly grown accustomed to living with. The house was dark and, for now, quiet. Alone with her thoughts, guilt consumed her - knowing what awaited her that day - she'd carefully shut herself off from the world. Tying up any loose ends without arousing suspicion in her family and friends. She knew that they cared, but even their love wasn't enough to pull her out of the hole she'd fallen into. Nothing mattered anymore, because at the other side of it all there was someone waiting for her. Her child. For years she'd gone through life with the short end of the stick, trailed by a string of bad luck that somehow, she'd always overcome, despite the emotional toll involved. This time was different, however. Her only begotten son was gone, a shock and blow that even her strong will couldn't absorb. On days when the liquor won, she would stumble through the house in a stupor. Drifting into the bedroom right next to her own, the woman would sit for hours inhaling the last scents of the child she'd never hold again. It was one of those days. Choking back a sob, she sank into the carpet, her eyes growing heavy as the pills she'd chased with whiskey began to go into effect. She knew that it was time; soon, she'd see her son again. Before she lost consciousness, a familiar voice rang throughout her head: "Mommy, please don't leave!" As she went under, she remembered the words, vowing to never leave his side again.

Chapter One

"He's gone! My only son, my baby is gone! Let me go! I'm not ready to leave! I can't abandon him!" I screamed as I was dragged away from the burial plot; my chic black pumps now spattered with specks of mud. The two men holding onto me were by no means physically weak, yet even they were struggling to restrain me. Unbeknownst to those sympathetically watching and the others gawking, I had made arrangements to stay until my son's casket was lowered into the ground and covered by the dirt that was currently shielded by the grass-colored green covering. The workers along with the remaining family members and nosy stragglers watched with odd glances at the scene that was taking place. Clearly, everyone thought I had finally snapped from the hurt of such a loss.

"Why won't they all just go the fuck away?!" I thought angrily. Watching me protest being forced inside of a waiting family limousine, Tracey attempted to calm my grieving soul assuring me that:

"You'll see him again one day. Be at peace knowing your son is with God in heaven. Even God had to watch Jesus die."

The words jarred me into submission. I snatched away from the men holding me and stood starkly upright. Staring from behind an expensive pair of darkly tinted Prada

shades, my red, swollen eyes shot daggers. If looks could kill, Tracey would have fallen dead right there at Houston Memorial Gardens, straight inside my child's freshly dug grave.

On any other day, I, Victoria Simone Gafford could light up a room with my presence. At five foot four my frame is brought to life by the unbothered confidence in my stride, while my youthful face held an infectious smile I'd come to be known for. With a sun kissed caramel skin tone that always seemed to glow and behind my almond shaped eyes hid a joke that only I seemed to know - a unique quirk that seemed to have a welcoming effect on those I came in contact with. Affectionately known by family and friends as simply Vee, on this day my round face held no trace of a smile. Stiffening my shoulders and casting a final longing glance in the direction of the workers completing this final part of their task I thought, maybe it's for the best that I do not remain for this. As my heart screamed in objection, I reluctantly stepped inside of the waiting limousine. I knew the tears would fall again, and soon, but for now I refused to let them drop, not today at least and definitely not in front of Tracey. That last week of January had started innocently enough, yet somehow became the most traumatizing of my life. I reluctantly agreed to go on a date with a man I met through a mutual associate. This absolutely wasn't the smartest idea. In fact, I could not have picked a worse time to stumble back into the dating pool. Just over three weeks ago, Eric – my former fiancé and father of my son - and I, had officially called it quits, ending a tumultuous relationship that we'd both grown weary of. For me, dating as an adult, was new frontier. I had not seriously considered a life that didn't include my high school sweetheart, Eric. A man I'd been inseparable with for years. He'd provided my first experience of love and inadvertently taught me that fairy tales don't always have a happy ending - at least, not mine anyway. Against my own better judgment, I agreed to the date, trying to convince myself that a simple night out would help dull the pain of my failed relationship. The doorbell rang as I gave myself a final check in the mirror. Approving of my reflection, I smoothed the wrinkles from my dress and admired the way my smooth skin glowed as I quickly headed over to my five-year-old's room to kiss him goodnight. Gently pushing open the door, my heart warmed at the sight of my mother affectionately reading a book of bible stories to the boy as he sat intently, hanging onto her every word. I reminisced about myself at that age, wondering if this is what it looked like when my mother would read these same stories to me. Not wanting to ruin the moment I called out softly, "Momma I'm headed out; I won't be out late."

Also named Victoria, my mother peered at me with a smile, "Ok Vee."

Jumping up with speed only a child seemed to possess, Colin leapt across the room and tumbled into my arms screaming "Mommy don't leave me!" His words knocked the wind out of me. I was already hesitant to go on the date; I had been fighting the strong urge to cancel all day. For days, Crystal had gushed about the man, but in this moment, I just wanted to be with my son. Looking down into his greenish-gray eyes, now filled with tears, I asked him softly.

 "What's wrong my love?"

Hugging me even tighter he answered,

"I just don't want you to go."

I was speechless.

In his short life Colin had never behaved this way before, and because of that, I decided to oblige him. Consoling my child, he finally began to calm down as the doorbell rang again. Now determined to go with my first mind, I pried my son from around my waist and made my way out of the room. Walking downstairs to open the front door, greet the person on the other side and officially nix the date. Coming up with an apology on the fly, I convinced my disappointed date to take a rain check on the evening, something he eagerly agreed to - though I had no clue whether that would actually happen. Right now, my mind was on Colin. Walking back into the house, I breathed a sigh of relief as I watched Keith's, my date, car pull out of the driveway. I knew I couldn't fool myself; it was entirely too soon. Slipping off my stiletto heels I began removing my earrings as I headed back up to Colin's room, telling myself that I would hold him extra close that night. What I didn't know however, was that it would be the last time I would do so.

January 25th is a date that will forever be imprinted on my mind. I woke up late this morning; flying through the house to get Colin dressed, so that I could sit him down in the living room with my father who would keep him occupied so I could get dressed as well. We were going to be late for church, a place I'd grown-up in, making my professional debut as a pianist there at the age of 11. As an adult church had also become a financial blessing, allowing me to earn a living by playing the piano every Sunday - rain or shine - at Concord Missionary Baptist Church.

Music is as much a part of me as my parents and Colin are. If I am in a bad mood, I will either lament my emotions with solemn tunes or cheer up with music that guided my emotions in the opposite direction. It's my outlet, especially when I was angry. I would literally take my frustrations out on the piano. Banging the keys similarly to how drummers bang drums. Percussion instruments are the best for reliving stress. Finally dressed, I rushed back into the living room to grab Colin. In the brief time it had taken me to lay my hair down and throw some clothes on, my child had somehow managed to create a masterpiece - a mess actually - with his finger paints. To him it was Rembrandt, worthy of hanging in the Houston Museum of Fine Arts or at least the refrigerator. But to me it was yet another obstacle in what was shaping up to be the morning from hell. At this rate I won't even leave the house, yet alone touching a piano. I am livid, more so at my father for allowing Colin to make the colorful mess. That was one of the cons of moving back into my childhood home, my son's grandparents were around constantly, indulging Colin's every desire. It is maddening, but I genuinely appreciate the love and support from my parents while I figured out my life, post Eric. In that moment I allowed my child to win, deciding to let Colin stay with my dad and finish what he'd started. I figured if I move quickly enough, I can still salvage the shitty morning. But that day

Colin wasn't having it, running over, and entangling himself in my legs as he'd done the night before.

Screaming "Mommy! Please don't leave me!" as the tears started to flow. But unlike the night before, this wasn't a date, and I couldn't miss work. There were bills that needed to be paid, and Colin was one of those bills. Unable to calm him down this time, I begrudgingly pried him from around my legs, scooping him up and placing him in my father's arms and then dashed out the door to head to church. Usually a bright and bubbly child, I thought. As I drove, Colin's tears and hysteria replayed over and over in my mind. It was so unlike him. My mind and my heart utterly conflicted as I could only see a tear drenched face as I backed out of the driveway. I contemplated returning home as I was turning into the parking lot. As I opened the door to get out of the vehicle, Colin's screaming as if his life depended on it, echoed in my mind. I turned around and grabbed my purse from the backseat. Kissing and hugging him tight, I transferred him into my father's waiting arms and exited the house; I shook my head at the thought and reminded myself that I had responsibilities to take care of. If I didn't show up, then I wouldn't be paid and unfortunately for us, I was no longer receiving an allowance from my parents. Hesitation mixed with weariness as I stepped away from the curb - entered the church and went to handle my business. Colin would understand one day...

And that's the last living memory that I have of my son. Not a day goes by that I don't fucking regret it. Had I known then what I know now....

As I am thumbing through my bible, searching to find the passage of scripture that the pastor just mentioned, when the church phone started ringing, which is slightly odd. Anyone with sense would know it'd be difficult to answer the call. We are too busy worshiping the Lord. Service was epic today! The choir went into extended praise and the music director put on a major performance. I was mentally giving myself a high five for the riffs and scales I added to some of the songs. Lately I'd started experimenting with infusing other genres of music into my playing. Not that I was being sacrilegious or anything like that. I wanted to diversify but my mother would always tell the story of Mahalia Jackson and how she turned down secular music to use her gift of singing for God only, every time I tried to talk to her about expanding my repertoire. So, I settled for sneaking in some jazz or blues chords for fun occasionally. For some odd reason, my heart skipped a beat as an usher hurried over my way, tapping me on the shoulder to come to the phone. In my gut, I knew that whoever it is on the other end, it couldn't be good.

"Hello?"

I half asked into the receiver once I reached the phone. It was my neighbor Steven; he was calling to inform me that emergency first responders were in front of my home and to come back right away. I dropped the phone down, telling the waiting usher to get my mother from the choir loft and inform her to meet me at my car. Immediately.

Sprinting out into the January air, my skin prickled as a chill swept across my body, but somehow, I knew it was more than the frigid air. Pacing on the side of my freshly washed Nissan Maxima, I couldn't help but feel annoyed as

I waited for my mother to exit the building. In that moment it seemed like forever. My mother stepped outside apprehensively and slightly annoyed that I had her leave service. I could hear the irritation in her voice when she asked,

"What's going on?"

She tried to hide it.

"I have no idea mommy; Steven called and said to hurry home now."

Thankfully, we live only five minutes away, I thought as we were on our way. I raced back to our neighborhood, speeding down North Main Street, breaking every traffic law imaginable in the process. Slowing down for the stop sign that sat in the intersection near my parents' home, I could see a gurney being pulled into a waiting ambulance. The lights somewhat blinding as the sirens pierced through the air. There were numerous police cars blocking the street and yellow tape was tied up marking out what appeared to be a crime scene. Immediately I thought of my father, my throat tightening as I imagined the possibility that something had happened to him. Colin hadn't crossed my mind. Nobody else crossed my mind. My daddy is 70 years old besides, no mother on the planet wants to believe the worst for her child and I am no different.

Pulling into the driveway of a neighbor's house, I barely managed to put the car in park before hopping out of the vehicle. Making my way to the ambulance, I froze as a voice called out "Is this the mother?" Instantly motionless, time seeming to stop as my body began to go numb. The crowd of first responders parted as I walked over to the group, giving me a view of the rear section of the ambulance: it wasn't my father. It was my brother, David. He'd been shot however the injury wasn't fatal. The ambulance and crew were gearing up to take David to the hospital. I turned to go into the house and that's when life as I knew it, was changed forever.

"Ma'am! Wait!"

A detective blocked my path and was trying to say something to me that I couldn't hear since sounds became muted and my eyes were fixated on the sight of a small frame laid on the gurney coming out of the front door.

Suddenly everything went black...

I have no clue how long I was blacked out, but when I came to, I was sitting on the ground and my mother was on her cell phone leaving a frantic message on Eric's voice mail. Eric Spencer - Colin's father - was already hard to reach by phone, and considering he wasn't a morning person on this day it was even harder. I don't have the patience for his nonsense. I angrily snatched the phone away from my mother as he answered groggily on the second ring. I was in a rage. Hysterically I screamed "Eric! Get the fuck up!! Get up!! Colin is in the hospital; he's been in an accident!! GET UP!!"

The ambulance headed to the hospital shortly after I fainted. My distraught older brother rode with them; my mother was concerned about and stayed with me. It seemed as if time had stopped as I waited for him to answer and by the time he did, I was livid. My mother was driving excruciatingly slow to the hospital. Neither one of us is in a good condition for driving, however at 70 years old; she's the lesser of two evils. I had never met anyone who moved as slowly as he did, but I thought today of all days he'd put a fucking pep into his step. But fear began to supersede my anger, my mother and I scrambling to Eric's car as he sped into the parking lot of Northwest Memorial Hermann Hospital.

After arriving we were immediately escorted to the back,

my eyes eagerly scanning the faces of the hospital staff for any clues or signs. Each face was solemn, causing my stomach to lurch and twist as I came to the dark realization that my son wouldn't be leaving the building in my arms. It was amazing to me just how many familiar faces I saw that day, in fact, one person even stopped me to ask what happened. The odd thing being that, that person had been sitting next to me at church when I received the call - meaning common sense should've told her that I knew about as much as she did. But then again, common sense isn't common.

Reaching Colin's hospital room, the doctor's voice sounded muffled and distorted, yet I heard him loud and clear as he explained to us that…

"The ventilator is basically keeping him alive. There are no vital readings without the machine. There's no brain activity at all."

"No! No… man, don't tell me that!" Eric screamed.

Slowly backing into the wall, he slid onto the floor. The doctor paused before uneasily moving towards the door, "I'll give you some time to decide what the next step is. I'm terribly sorry."

As the doctor exited the room, I stared blankly at my baby lying in the hospital bed. His chest rising and falling, and the last five years of his life flashed before my eyes: The baby shower and the support from Tamika, Eric's sister, who'd taken pride in feeding me - graciously indulging my pregnancy whims and cravings. Over the years she'd become like a sister to me, as well. I thought of my mother, who'd held my hand through the painful labor as I gave birth. I remembered holding my son for the first time and falling in love after looking into his hypnotic greenish, gray eyes. I thought of Colin's first words. His first steps. The sound of his laughter. Memories of good times with Eric, moving into our first apartment as a family. Colin's first time saying, "I love you Mama." I remembered it all. My mind traveled back to when Colin was first born. Eric and I were not on good terms at all. We weren't even speaking. The phone in my hospital room rang and it was Eric. "Hey, can I come up?" I know the only person who could've told him what hospital we were at, was his sister, at that time she was like a sister to me as well; my irritation subsided quickly since a part of me was glad that he came. "Why do you want to see a baby you don't think is yours?" I was being an asshole, but I didn't care, I wasn't going to let him get off that easily after hurting me. "Can I come up or not?" This was typical of him, once he's over something then that should be the end of it. Begrudgingly I said yes and a few minutes later, in walks Eric and to my appalled surprise he wasn't alone. "Wassup Vee!" Ray exclaimed with a huge grin on his face. My hair was all over my head, my face was slightly swollen, and I wasn't feeling my best wearing a flimsy hospital gown. Ray took one look at Colin and turned to his best friend "So what are you going to name your son?" This is how our son acquired his name. "He looks like a white baby, man look at her and look at me, this isn't even her baby" we all burst into laughter and "white boy" Colin became his name. My heart aching as I realized there wouldn't be any more memories. No new ones anyway. My son, my baby was gone. Forever. "Vee, VEE!"

I was snatched out of my daze and back to the present as Eric desperately called my name. "We have to make a decision." *Make a decision about what*, I wondered. Dazed and confused, I hadn't realized that night had fallen. Still in shock, apparently, I'd been in a trance for hours. Eric pressed on, "He's not functioning on his own, and the machine is doing everything for him. We have to let him go. And we have to consent to turn it off."

"What the fuck do you mean?" I hissed.

We were young parents just trying to figure it out. I, being only 21 while Eric was 23 years old. We were still growing up ourselves and now life is escalating the process. We had barely gotten the hang of balancing Colin's needs with our wants. Hell, we had just come to an agreement on what school he would go to in the fall. The argument over that, seemed pointless and pathetic now. Eric wanted him at the popular school, and I was focused on higher level education. Strange how death seems to always reveal what really matters in life. How in the world did they expect us to give consent to turn off the damn ventilator? We were barely out of childhood our damn selves. I don't want to let him go. I don't want to even be here. I am not ready to accept that our only child is dead. Already irate, I was quickly becoming belligerent as I lashed out at Colin's father.

"I'm not consenting to a got damn thing!"

Looking around my son's hospital room, the faces staring

back at me all shared a similar look; a unique blend of sadness and pity, the latter only further infuriating me. I don't want fucking pity; I want my son back. Finally, I snapped, kicking every single soul out of the room: "Everybody. Get. The. Fuck. out. Now."

I stood coldly as the room emptied, finally climbing into bed with Colin, his body now barely lukewarm. He didn't move. Couldn't move. He didn't snuggle into my side like he normally did. His breathing moved with a labored rhythm, but it was being produced artificially. It wasn't his natural pattern anymore that much I knew. Defeated, I began to wonder what had I done in life to deserve this? Why has God forsaken me? I began to accept that my baby is gone. The tears started flowing and I know that they won't stop anytime soon. The door opened slowly as Eric and Colin's physician came back into the room.

"It's time," Eric whispered.

He hugged me tight as I shook my head no, vehemently. I wasn't ready and didn't think I would ever be ready. Not for this. Hot tears fell on top of my head before Eric finally pulled me away from Colin, composing himself as the doctor handed me a clipboard. Scanning the consent forms, I saw that Eric had already signed the consent papers - and in that moment I hated him. After reluctantly writing my signature next to his, I handed the clipboard over to Colin's doctor, who continued to apologize and offer his condolences. Gathering both of our families together, Pastor Kerry Williams instructed everyone to re-enter the room, grasp hands and form a circle around us. His smooth baritone voice leading a prayer that seemed to calm everyone, except me. In fact, rage that was quickly becoming familiar had begun to rise inside of me. With every benevolent request he made to God for our strength, inwardly I felt like a petulant child throwing a tantrum because I couldn't get my way. I refuse to close my eyes. I refuse to pretend to feel anything by calling out 'amen' with the rest of them. Fuck that.

Slowly, as everyone was exiting the room one by one, in that moment I defiantly vowed to give God the silent treatment for the rest of my natural life. I had never felt such hurt or betrayal - it was a pain I felt on a spiritual and physical level - not understanding how God could abandon someone he allegedly loves so much.

To their credit, the nurses did their best to ease the process for me. Entering the room silently, one nurse took my hand, leading me to a rocking chair I somehow hadn't noticed before. Physically and mentally exhausted, I sank into the chair as a series of beeps and pulses served as the only noise in the room. Each click of a button furthered the process of disconnecting the breathing machine. And each click felt like a gunshot to my heart, as I died a little with each sound. Once he was completely disconnected - that's what they called it "disconnected," as if dressing up the word made it any less ugly - Colin was swaddled in a blanket and gently placed in my arms. In that moment, the record scratched. It was surreal. This was the same way that Colin had been presented to me at birth, his first day of life. Now on his last day, everything had come full circle. I wept bitterly. For Colin. For his future and all the other things, he'd never get to do or experience. For the future memories we would never make. For the rocky beginning that he was born in… I rocked and hugged him close, refusing to accept that his small arms would never hug me back again. A blood curdling scream bubbled up and escaped from my lips. My soul ached. Shit, everything ached. So, I cried until my eyes dried out, and then I cried again. Eventually, my body went numb, and I couldn't feel anything. I thought that I had died as well. In fact, I wished that I had.

Eric

The phone just wouldn't stop ringing, the sound cutting through his sleep as he struggled to ignore it. Exhausted, it was way too early for his phone to be ringing like this. Turning over he mumbled "Vee answer the pho..." before cutting himself off. So accustomed to her being near his side, it was something he still wasn't used to. Angrily scooping up the phone, he groggily answered with "What!" He knew the voice on the other end well but had never heard it laced with so much panic, making him unable to hear anything other than high pitched screaming mixed with vulgarities - which only irritated him more. It was too early for Vee's shit. Looking at the screen he wondered why she wasn't at church. Shouldn't she be playing that piano she loved so fucking much? Tired and eager to cut the conversation short he started with "Vee...VEE! Calm yo ass down. Wha..."

Quickly cutting him off, he sat dumbstruck as she uttered the words that would forever change his life: "Colin is in the fucking hospital!! Get your ass the fuck up and come meet us!! Northwest Memorial!! Hurry up!!!"

"What's wrong with him?"

"Can you please just for once think about someone other than yourself and get your lazy ass up now!!!"

Eric hung up the phone. Vee could be so damn dramatic. She was probably panicking over him sneezing too many times. Parenting hadn't come with an instruction manual and at 23; he and Vee had just gotten to the point where they could consider themselves a family - until last week at least. Climbing out of bed, he began to get dressed, trying to convince himself that Vee was simply overreacting. Still struggling to wake up, he'd assumed she'd said, "Colin needs to be picked up from the hospital," not that he was actually in the hospital. Soon he'd realize just how wrong he'd been.

******

As Eric slowly slid down the wall to the floor, the entire morning flashed in his mind with brutal alarm. Every action he had made was now added to a list of regrets that would haunt him for eternity. Eric now hated himself for ignoring his phone, turning the ringer on vibrate, taking his time about getting to Victoria when she called. He willed himself to believe that this was all a nightmare, however watching the first woman he'd ever loved, the mother of his only son, scream hysterically and sink to her knees in utter anguish forced to him realize that he had actually been told that his son, his junior, his best friend, his only baby boy… is dead. He sat on the floor in a daze, until he noticed a multitude of feet. He shook his head to clear his vision and looked up into numerous faces, most of which he didn't even recognize. Who in the hell are these people?! Eric got up off the floor, he needed space. He quietly exited the room and leaned against the nurses' station to gather himself.

"Can I get you some water or something else to drink?" Eric turned towards the nurse and shook his head when his voice failed him. A heavy hand rested on his shoulder and Eric turned around to face the doctor who had just given them the horrible news.

"Can I speak with you, Mr. Spencer?"

"It's Eric… yeah, sure."

Eric followed the doctor into a quiet room down the hallway.

"I'm speaking with you first, since your wife doesn't seem receptive to… there's some paperwork that needs to be signed by the both of you and it's my opinion that the transition is easier when a spouse or the parent assists."

We aren't married... She's not my wife... That's all she wanted and that's the reason she left him. "We both come from married parents and our son isn't deserving of married parents?!" It was the last thing Vee said to him before she moved out. He shook his head trying to process what the doctor was telling me.

"Assists?... with what?"

"These papers are in regard to removing your son from life support. I…"

"What the fuck do you mean remove my son from life support?"

Eric could feel his rage and anger beginning to boil over.

"Mr. Spencer, it is with much regret that I inform you that your son is not functioning on his own nor will he ever have the capabilities to do so any longer. He's already gone, and the machine is literally acting as a puppet master. Colin has no brain activity at all. It is however you and your wife's choice to keep your son connected to the device but just know that you would ultimately cause yourself more anguish and grief. I'll give you a few moments alone."

The doctor exited the room and left Eric alone with his thoughts. Eric stared at the papers and thought about what the doctor said. Life was so strange. Eric had always made a point to correct anyone that referred to Victoria as his wife and not once had he corrected the doctor. A couple weeks ago, he and Victoria were actively trying to have another baby; a little girl is what they hoped for. They were all under the same roof… now here he was having to swallow that not only had he lost the woman he loved, now his son and only connection to her is gone as well. As long as Colin was alive, there was hope for… no point in having hope anymore. Eric picked up the pen and signed his name on the highlighted blanks as his tears saturated his face and his soul shriveled and died as well. Between the alcohol, lack of sleep, an affinity for drank and sheer anger, the days following Colin's death were a blur. Eric still didn't have a good enough explanation for why he was no longer a father, that alone fueled his rage to extreme levels. Fuck seeing red, he wanted to kill somebody. Someone needed to atone for the death of his son. To feel the pain that he felt. Instead, he found ways to distract himself from the emotional pain; straddling so many lines he wondered how he kept managing to evade jail. A detective kept calling and leaving messages, but Eric didn't want to talk to the cops about anything, they should call Victoria. If she would've had her ass at home where she belonged, then their son would still be alive...

Had he been honest with himself, he would've acknowledged that his pain was laced with guilt. In addition, the rage, it was the only other thing he seemed to feel nowadays. Guilt for suggesting Vee get an abortion when he first found out she was pregnant. Guilt for how coldly he'd treated her during the pregnancy. For not coming to the hospital until after he was born, giving Colin his name only to turn around and demand a paternity test. Guilt for taking his time to meet her at the hospital the morning that he died. But it was easier to point the finger at someone else, and in time that finger would land squarely on Vee.

The blaring car horn brought him out of the hazy fog of in his mind.

Lost in his thoughts, the sound of a horn brought him back to the present. Opening the front door, Eric was blinded by the sun. He didn't even know what day it was. Pulling his cap down lower, he shut the door behind him and made his way towards the car where his brother from another mother was waiting. Not only was Ray his best friend, but he was also Colin's godfather and now, the only person that Eric had spoken to or allowed around him.

Ray didn't ask him how he felt or try to force any information out of him, instead, knowing that Eric needed time to ride and drink like they used to before they became adults - and parents. Like they used to back when they were still adolescents without a care in the world. A sprawling city, they'd been driving around Houston for the past hour with no destination in mind. He just needed to think. The sound of his phone ringing caused him to look down with disdain. It was Vee calling, again. Reluctantly answering the phone, he immediately noticed that she sounded as lifeless as he felt.

"Eric, we have an appointment at the funeral home tomorrow morning at nine. Are you picking me up or meeting me there?"

"I really don't want to go at all. Is your mom going?"

A defeated sigh escaped her lips as she replied, "No Eric, why would she? She's not his parent, we are."

"I'm not going."

"I hate you."

"The feeling is mutual sweetheart."

He instantly felt remorse as Vee hung up in his face. He knew that she didn't deserve to be treated like this but hell; he wasn't ready to deal with it either. He willed his mind to go blank as he poured another cup of drank - a mixture of promethazine, codeine, and today's soda of choice Mountain Dew - that usually relaxed him. Lately, it had no impact at all. Ray was concerned about his friend. He usually steered clear of whatever went on between Eric and Vee, but the death of their son had made their relationship borderline toxic. He couldn't even begin to understand what his best friend - more like a brother - was going through. Hell, none of their friends could, they were all kids practically themselves. Their entire crew made up early twenty somethings; a few had children the same age as Colin, but most had none. For the first time in days Ray finally brought up the elephant in the room.

"Have you talked to your girl?"

silence

"Say man, you hear me" he chuckled.

"Yeah, that was her that just called. She's going to the mortuary in the morning."

"What time?"

silence

"Are you going bro?"

"Nah man, turn the music back up."

Sensing he wouldn't get any further, at least not today, Ray turned the music back up. Navigating through Houston's notoriously congested Galleria area; the duo rode down Highway 59 in silence as they headed back to 5th Ward. Eric didn't want to feel anything. Didn't want to feel any pressure, or answer questions, or deal with that nagging hurt. Eric looked down at his ringing phone, this time it was his sister Tamika.

"Yeah, Tam what's up?"

"Have you talked to Vee, she's not answering my calls or calling me back and we need to know if services have been planned…"

"Man, I don't know. I don't have anything to do with that."

"What do you mean…?"

"Look don't call me with this bullshit alright!"

Eric contemplated throwing the device out the car window. Instead, he just turned it completely off and dropped it onto the floor.

Victoria

" Vee, are you sure that you don't want me to go?" My mother, affectionately called Dodie by close family only, was worried about her baby girl. She wanted to help but was unsure where to start. How do you console your child…about the death of her child? Some situations you're just never prepared for. Trying to sound brave for my mother, I replied "I'll be ok mommy." Neither one was doing a good job of convincing the other. Hugging my mother tightly, I then proceeded to walk out the door, pulling it shut and locking it behind me. Now on the other side, I faintly heard my mother sobbing. My heart felt like cement in my chest. How much more would I have to endure?

The closer I got to my destination the more intense my anxiety became. By the time I reached Pruitt's Mortuary I was in full panic mode, parking and practically falling out of the car in an attempt to catch my breath. Devon, a former coworker from my days employed by the mortuary - slowly walked up and pulled me into an embrace - staying that way until I finally began to breathe normally again. As we entered the building my knees slightly buckled, but with Devon's assistance I made it to the conference room. I made it through the meeting in a mostly robotic state - during which I'd barely spoken, saying either "no" or "yes" as needed. Had it been left up to me alone, they would had held a graveside service for immediate family only and be done with it. Even in this moment I was still being considerate of everyone else's feelings and wants. While working together here, Devon and I had developed a genuine friendship, and it was he who persuaded me to at least have a memorial service the Friday night before the graveside service that Saturday morning. Once the details had been set, I made another appointment to bring in the clothes that Colin would be buried in. I had been unprepared thanks in part to the medical examiner, who'd only released his body to the mortuary that morning. Not wanting to push the boundaries of our friendship, I debated whether, to ask what I knew would be considered an outlandish request - and also one that could potentially get him in trouble. But in the end, I threw caution to the wind, shooting a shot in the dark and hoping for the best.

****

"Devon... please let me see him."

Her voice was barely a whisper, he wasn't sure if he'd actually heard her. But once he turned around and saw that Victoria was no longer following him to the front, he knew that he had heard her correctly. Wanting to help but knowing he could not, it broke his heart to say...

"No, Vee I can't do that, and you shouldn't want to see him like that. You know how M.E. cases come…"

"Please… I just want to hold him one last time."

"I ca…"

"I need this. I feel so empty. So, lost."

Her face flooding with tears as she sank to the floor in a heap of herself and her belongings. Devon came back to her and sat next to her on the floor. Gathering her into his arms, she just continued to sob despondently. Unable to give her what she wanted, instead Devon came up with an idea to bend regulations rather than break them altogether - and if it helped his friend heal - it was worth it.

****

Facing me he said, "When you bring his clothes on Thursday, after I do the major work, I'll let you help dress him."

Words couldn't adequately express my gratitude, instead I hugged him tightly. After a moment he helped me off the floor and picked up my bag. He kept his arm around my shoulders as he escorted me out of the door and to my car. After saying our goodbyes, he watched me drive away.

I couldn't figure out which was more intense, the hurt over losing my son or the brewing hatred towards his father,

Eric.

How could the one person on the planet that should empathize with me, that knew exactly what I was going through, be so cruel and unkind? In addition to leaving all our child's funeral arrangements to me, including choosing his final outfit, on the night of Colin's memorial service he refused to ride with me to the church.

"Where are you? The car will be here any minute."

"I'm driving myself."

"So, you're picking me up?"

"No."

"Why would you do this?"

"I don't…."

Ending the conversation, I shook my head in an effort to dismiss it from my mind. At this point I'd had enough. Whatever feelings I had left for Eric were officially dead, along with our son. He'd never been the epitome of the perfect boyfriend; however, a part of me had always hoped he could be. Love can be a painful bitch, especially when given to the wrong person. But after investing so much time into another person, leaving the relationship can make you feel like a failure - something that had kept both of us around for a while. In our case however, neither parent was interested in fighting anymore. Not with each other, and certainly not for our relationship.

Eric

Eric looked at himself in the mirror for a final time, carefully putting on his hat before heading out the door to join his family in an awaiting limousine. He hated funerals. This one would definitely be no exception. No parent should ever have to bury their own child. Their only child. He looked down at the DVD case he held tightly in his right hand, beads of sweat beginning to form across his knuckles as they began to turn white, his eyes watering up as he read the title for what felt like the millionth time. Finding Nemo.

It was Colin's favorite movie, often on a continuous loop that played from the time he woke up to the time he went to bed at night - driving both Vee and him crazy. Remembering a time, they tried to hide the video from Colin brought a slight smile to his face as he loosened up his grip. Times weren't always bad. They couldn't have been, considering they were trying to conceive another child before their lives fell apart...

They arrived at the church to find all their family members in various shades of blue. Eric's face flushed as he instantly became annoyed. He should be in blue as well, but of course Vee hadn't bothered to call and tell him personally. She'd made sure to tell everyone else though, he thought bitterly. Vee could be so selfish and childish, conveniently overlooking how selfish and childish he could be as well. All she wanted was him and their family and he wasn't ready to settle down. Hell, he was only 21 when she finally graduated high school and he couldn't understand how at 18 she wanted to get married. Victoria wanted to get married, move in together, raise their child together and have another baby together. I wasn't ready for all that responsibility. I loved being Colin's dad and I loved Vee and I wanted a baby girl with her so I could have a version of her for the rest of my life but not on her timeline. Eric's thoughts of her irritated him yet when he walked into the church, she was the first one he searched the room for, making his way upstairs to the second floor when he didn't find her on the first floor. He didn't have to look far, immediately seeing her as he reached the top of the stairs. She looked absolutely beautiful, especially when she was angry, though he had enough sense - and pride - not to say so. Anger he could deal with versus her hurt. He didn't know how to process his own pain, let alone hers. Usually so resilient, the sight of her tears made him feel oddly inadequate. Their eyes met and Eric was completely sure in that moment that she wished him death as well based on the rage in her beautiful eyes. He didn't say a word, choosing instead to walk up and grab her hand. Handing her the DVD, he led her into the sanctuary where their son's casket had been placed for viewing. Vee stopped in her tracks once she realized where he was taking her, not yet ready to face what they were all there for. Gently but firmly pulling her hand, what Vee didn't know was that Eric couldn't approach their son's casket without her. They would need to lean on each other for strength, but Victoria's pride wouldn't allow her to admit that she needed him too. A double-edged sword, on one hand his pride had allowed him to cope with Colin's death the best he could, on the other it caused him to hurt a woman that still meant the world to him. But allowing Vee to see his hurt would force him to admit the truth, that this wasn't a horrible nightmare after all, it was now their reality.

Victoria

Despite assurances from family and friends that "the ceremony was beautiful," the entire funeral had been a blur for me. To be honest I didn't give a damn. I appreciated the kind words and swell of support, but the reality of the situation was finally starting to sink in: no matter how hard I prayed, cried out loud or even ignored God, Colin wasn't coming back. It was a brutal truth my 21-year-old mind and spirit wasn't emotionally or mentally equipped to handle. Few people were.

Then there was Eric.

Already strained, the death of Colin had stretched the fabric of our relationship to its limits, further estranging the former lovers. Distraught with his own grief, I had been left to plan our child's funeral alone, going through the motions as I threw my energy into details like the coffin, headstone, and outfit he would ultimately rest in. I didn't have the luxury of grieving because there was simply no one else to handle the details. If Colin's father couldn't pull it together, his mother, for damn sure would.

The equivalent of a robot, somehow, I made it through the ceremony, staring stonily out the window as my family's limousine carefully rounded a curve on the way to the repass. Things were so tense that Eric and his family had rode separately, using our large entourages as a cover for taking two limousines.

Right now, I couldn't stand the sight of him since he'd essentially abandoned me. I couldn't stand the way he'd somehow managed to make himself the focal point at the memorial service, looking dapper but appearing in completely the wrong color. Had he taken the time to listen to me or at least help share the final responsibilities, he would've known everyone was wearing blue.

Why should I have to beg him to listen to me? Both of our

families had worn some form of blue because that was the color that Colin was dressed in. It seems odd that I was able to function so efficiently despite neglecting all my other responsibilities. My baby looked like a model. I dressed him in a blue sweater vest with ombre' effect, long sleeve white button up shirt, dark blue linen pants and fresh all white S. Carters. Then there was Eric's former girlfriend, who showed up dressed as if she was entering a nightclub, then had the audacity to bump into me by "accident." A petty move that got the woman escorted out of the church and caused Eric to lash out, accusing me of being childish and immature. "Why are you causing a scene? This isn't about you!" Eric's verbal attack was just another bullet point on a long list of infractions where he's never had my back. I thought about the beginnings of my pregnancy and this same girl was telling everybody that I had an abortion or that I had a miscarriage because my stomach was too flat to be pregnant. Fast forward here we are years later at my son's funeral like she had been praying for it or something.

"Fuck you and that horse faced, bad built bitch, you're welcome to join her on the other side of that door for all I care."

A few of Eric's acquaintances only made it worse after they asked to take pictures of Colin - in his casket - a callous tacky request that drove me ballistic and I stormed out of the building. Not surprisingly, no one followed me, which was fine. I was becoming thoroughly accustomed to having my own back. Angry, numb, and drained, once we arrived at the repast site I settled into a chair in the corner, fighting the urge to put my head down on the table and cry; I watched bitterly as everyone around the room seemingly celebrated my son's life. I understand, Lord knows I do, but I am angry. Furious even. This isn't a party. My child is dead, yet I knew that life would continue to go on, and that's what pissed me off the most.

I heard a voice call out, "Hey girl! I'm about to leave, but I'd like you to meet someone special."

Raising my eyes to meet hers, I summed up the woman that stood before me. Shameka, my closest friend... She has been quite honestly, missing in action as of late. I stared blankly, not quite comprehending how I am supposed to play nice and make small talk with a stranger on the hardest day of my life. Meka had a history for being slightly callous and supercilious at times, something I couldn't help but remember in that moment.

I flashed back to the car crash we were involved in when I was eight months pregnant, the result of a distracted Meka anxious to get her boyfriend's house. Just along for the ride, it was one that I - and Colin - almost didn't survive after Meka smashed into the back of a truck. In her haste to get to that young man's house she'd ignored my request to visit an ER, leaving me to sit outside in the car once we finally arrived at her desired destination. There'd been other red flags throughout the years, but I found it difficult to pull the plug on a friendship first started by our families in their youth. Shaking the past from my mind I answered,

"Hey, nice to meet you."

My tone of voice was utterly dry.

Slowly standing up, I offered my hand to Meka's newest guy. My face was suddenly hot as I willed myself to calm the surge of annoyance that was growing inside of me. Humans are curious creatures; an unfortunate fact I often reminded myself of. Too tired to acknowledge my alleged best friend's blatant disregard of the obvious bad timing, instead I excused myself and made my way across the room - filing the encounter away for a later time.

Now was not the time because today - it was all about Colin.

****

I made my way to the mailbox. I wasn't looking for anything in particular, but it was a routine - one of many - that I learned to rely on in the days and weeks since the funeral. All I could do was take it day by day. It was the kind of cliché advice I learned to hate, but heed, nonetheless. Lost in my thoughts, I opened and shut the box, thumbing through the mail before stopping in my tracks; I carefully examined the invitation in my hand, a flowery creation sent by her estranged best friend. My fingers traced the slightly raised lettering, Shameka Anderson's name shining brightly in gold. I wasn't angry, quite the contrary actually, but I couldn't help but wonder just when our friendship had derailed to the point that I had to discover a life milestone via the U.S. Postal Service. Had we ever been friends at all? Looking back, it was highly unlikely. I was just space filler for Meka's narcissism. I was unsure of how I felt, in fact; I was tired of feeling shit altogether. Something inside of me clicked...

I grabbed my keys from the bar and hopped into my ride and headed towards 610 and Lockwood. I'd spent a lot of my childhood in the Trinity/Kashmere Gardens area. On the weekends, I stayed with my big sister at her house on Peachtree St for Sunday Fundays in Busby Park. I graduated from the illustrious Barbara Jordan High School. That's where Eric and I met. My thoughts jumbled together as I finally turned into the driveway. I turned the car off and just stared at the house that held so many memories... good and bad. I remember when we finally moved in. I was happy and content living on the East side in our "luxury townhouse". I laughed slightly at how I thought we were really accomplished to be that young living in non-subsidized accommodations. An opportunity to move back to the hood presented itself and typical Eric, breaks our lease to move into this very house, so that he could be "closer to this granny" was what he said. I knew he just wanted to be closer to his friends. I stepped back into the home that Eric and I technically still shared. I was rarely here, opting to spend most of my time at my mother's house, returning only because the house was closer to my school's campus. I had rushed to register for classes even though my initial motivation was gone. Initially I returned back to college to make a better life for myself and Colin - but now that he was gone, I simply needed a distraction because day and night, he is all I think about. To my relief Eric wasn't here yet, making what I was about to do even easier - or so I thought. My eyes grazed the interior as I made my way upstairs, gathering and packing my things for the final time. It hurt to go into Colin's room: to see his toys with the knowledge that he'd never get to play with them again. It really fucking hurt. However, I was tired. Everyone and everything had control over my life except me. That would end, starting now.

Nowadays Eric and I rarely even spoke to one another and when we did, we argued every single time. I was starting to feel suffocated. It was more weight on top of the already heavy burden I was carrying and despite Eric's pleas for me to stay, in my heart I knew the relationship was over.

Downstairs the front door opened and closed, signaling that

Eric had finally made it home. Parking my car in the driveway, I'd made no effort to conceal that I was here - and Eric knew exactly what I was here for. His steps echoed through the hall as he made his way upstairs, making a beeline for our son's room. Stepping inside, his eyes zeroed in on me as I finished putting Colin's favorite stuffed animal into an overnight bag.

"So, you're moving out?" he asked.

I wasn't ready for the confrontation I knew lay ahead, quietly praying that the conversation could be salvaged before it went left.

"I think it's for the best..."

Eric

Shock and joy invaded his heart as he turned into the driveway and saw Victoria's car parked there. As of late he would come home to evidence that she'd been there, which made him believe she was purposely coming when he wasn't there. Sometimes he would linger around in hopes to catch her, but she even had a plan for that, going to his sister's house across the street until he finally gave up and left. He really couldn't blame her for avoiding him, but he did anyway. Shutting the car off, joy turned into anger. He entered the house determined to have this much needed conversation while getting answers to his questions in the process. Stepping inside he almost tripped over a suitcase left half-open near the door, answering one of his questions in the process. He instantly became irate - it wasn't the answer he wanted. Eric knew that things had changed between them, but the history between them was enough to make him want to hold on, or at least put up one last fight for the road. He was ready for the challenge.

"So, you weren't going to say anything? You said that we would talk about it. That you just needed space and would be back."

Standing up she explained,

"Don't do this. Don't make it ugly. We both know what it was when you abandoned me when I needed you the most. So, I'm just taking the things that I bought for Colin, I'm getting my stuff and I'm moving back into my mom's house."

"Oh okay," he replied… Then all hell broke loose.

Victoria

I am tired of fighting. I am tired of struggling against the waves of emotions that swept over me daily. I just wanted to grab our things and go. Stepping around him, I was eager to leave and close this painful chapter as best I could. Making my way downstairs I moved as quickly as I could, ready to pack our things into the car and go. Zipping the suitcase closed I yanked open the front door, sunlight spilling into the dark living room that hadn't been cleaned in days. The love was gone in this house, of that, I was sure. Eric had other plans, grabbing our belongings, and throwing them right onto the lawn. My face flushed at the disrespect, my body running hot as I watched things like Colin's clothes and toys fly through the morning air. I'd had enough, screaming "What the fuck are you doing? What in the hell is wrong with you? Why are you doing this? The nerve of you! After everything I put up with! After everything you put me through!"

Angry and ashamed, I wanted to throw the entire day away. Throw the whole fucking year away. I struggled to shove everything into the car, picking Colin's things up off the ground - where his own father had flung them like garbage. The fucking disrespect. Our son's body was barely cold in the overpriced coffin I'd picked out alone, yet here his parents were, putting on a full show on the front lawn.

And put on a show we did, as Eric growled.

"Fuck this and fuck you."

"Fuck me? FUCK ME? You didn't even want our son, but now it's fuck me? Fine." I am tired in every sense of the word... And with Colin gone, the last tie holding Eric and I together has been broken. In some ways, I was glad. My child's father wasn't done either. Calling out,

"Get your shit and get the fuck out my yard." His words cutting far deeper than any physical act could.

"Your yard?!" I asked.

Anger and hatred mixing outside of the home we'd once happily shared.

"I hate I ever had a child with you. In fact, I hate I ever met your ass. Your selfish ass abandoned me to do EVERYTHING by. My. Muthafucking. Self! While you're off riding around doing nothing as usual, I had to go buy a plot of dirt for our son to be placed in! I had to go to the funeral home by myself! I had to buy his clothes! I had to deal with detectives and CPS!!"

Not to be outdone, with a final nail in the coffin Eric added

"I don't give a fuck, you heard what I said, bitch. Get your shit and get the fuck on. I hate that you had him too. He'd still be alive if you weren't his mama. So yeah, I hate you more...selfish bitch."

And there it was. I felt as if someone had hit me directly in the chest with a sledgehammer. My lungs collapsed; at least that's what it felt like. I was struggling to breathe. Picking the last of Colin's belongings off the ground, I finally got inside of my car. As I pulled off, I refused to look back into the rear-view mirror. It was officially over. I didn't know what was ahead, but I damn sure wasn't going back.

Chapter Two

"Victoria!"

"Ma'am?"

She got up to see what her mother was calling for her. Sitting at her desk with an envelope, Dodie looked up at her baby girl as Vee approached. She was still as beautiful as the day she'd been born, but that light inside of her, the one that used to command an entire room, was diminished. In the months following her grandson's death, she'd watched her daughter slowly transform into a person she barely recognized. As a mother, it hurt not to be able to fix what was broken instead, all she could do was pray even harder for Jesus to protect her child, put her back together, and/or at least give her child some peace.

"You called me momma?"

"Do you have any plans today?" Dodie asked, even though she already knew the answer to her question. Vee had quickly enrolled in school a few weeks after the funeral and quietly dropped out shortly after. Now, Dodie just wanted to treat her daughter with some semblance of normalcy in hopes of bringing her back to life.

"No ma'am"

"Ok, I'd like for you to drive me somewhere. I have to go to an office building in Greenway Plaza."

"Ok momma, I'll go get dressed."

As Vee slowly exited the room, it was all Dodie could do to keep herself from crying - during this trying time in their lives, her daughter's strength was awe inspiring. Even though she didn't need to be alone, Vee had all but pushed Dodie out the door and back to work; staying secluded in her room in an effort not to burden anyone with her grief. Yes, she was incredibly strong, but this was the terrible downside of that strength.

More often than not now, Dodie overate just to make sure

she saw her daughter eat something to offset all of the liquor she was consuming. Something Victoria thought her mother was unaware of. She quietly sent up a 'thank you' to the Holy Trinity once she heard the shower turn on, the pounding of the water briefly replacing all sounds in the otherwise quite house. After Dodie had to bathe Vee one night, she'd made her daughter promise to at least bathe once every couple of days. I didn't want to be here; however, when the one person that has never left your side asks you to accompany her…

 you can't tell your mother, no.

We entered an incredibly tall building that required two elevators just to reach our destination, the 24th floor. As we approached the heavy glass doors, I noticed "The Law Offices of Glenn Patterson" in big sprawling gold letters across the wall. I held the door open for my mommy and took a seat as she went to speak with the receptionist, confidently strolling to the front. At 70 years old, Dodie didn't look a day over 50. Her light beige skin always glowed. She wore her salt and pepper hair short and curly. She was always fashionably dressed, especially for church. I admired my mommy so much. I'd always hoped to be a mother just like her… however, that was no longer in the cards for me.

Roughly five minutes later, an older Caucasian gentleman with striking white hair appeared, coming out to greet my mother and me. After inviting my mother to a conference room in the back, she motioned for me to join them - I wasn't in a good space to deal with other people, but I obliged my mother - I knew she was genuinely concerned, and I didn't want to worry her even more than I already had.

"Hello Victoria, I apologize for the circumstances under which we are meeting today, however, I'm glad to finally make your acquaintance. I want to first introduce myself; my name is Glenn Patterson, and everyone calls me Pat. We're here today because your mother contacted me on your behalf to inquire about options to help relieve some of your stress. I'm an attorney that focuses on personal injury and other civil matters."

And there it was. My mother had brought me here to file a lawsuit in the death of my child. I was instantly offended - hurt and angry simultaneously as I glared at my mother. Her facial expression was soft and hesitant as she silently pleaded for understanding. My head snapped back in Mr. Patterson's direction as he called my name again, daggers shooting from my eyes. His tone was empathetic as he told me "It's your decision whether to move forward or not. There's no ill will on anyone's part. Your mother just felt that if there was some type of responsibility taken in your son's death, then maybe you could start the healing process. No one should have to go through what you're experiencing, especially at your age."

I sat there in a daze as I contemplated what he'd just said. With a heavy sigh I nodded my head yes. Opening a file folder, he handed me a stack of forms to complete.

Shaking hands as my mother and I prepared to leave, Mr. Patterson informed me that he would be sending me to a therapist, effective the next day. "We'll send a car to pick you up and bring you back home, so you won't have to worry about transportation" he promised. Adding, "Lunch will be included." With a hushed "ok" I escaped from the room. During the drive home I sat angrily, glancing between my mother's worried face and back out the window. I didn't always understand her, but now that I'd experienced motherhood, if only briefly, I fully understood the desire to protect your child, no matter the circumstances.

****

"Do you want this woman to be your mother?"
It was the same dream I had every time my anxiety peaked.
A vivid image of my younger self standing between my
parents as we all stood inside of a courtroom in a front of a
judge…

I opened one eye and looked at the clock. It was 3:43 am but despite the late hour I was alert and wide awake. Dragging myself out of bed, I fished around for my slippers, avoiding the cold floor by shoving my toes into the warm, insulated shoes. Last night was the first time in a long time that I had tried to sleep without the aid of alcohol, drank or pills; as a result, I'd tossed and turned, only getting about an hour of sleep.

I was fairly sure my memories were haunting me because of yesterday's events. Quietly making my way outside to the back porch, I sat down, finding a familiar comfort on my favorite swing. In order to fend off the urge to fix myself a glass of something, I thought about the meeting with the therapist later that morning. I thought counselors, psychiatrists; therapists and anyone else that made a habit of screwing around in people's heads is manipulative people that preyed on the naivety of others - essentially taking advantage of people who were down in a moment of weakness. Like many others within the Black community, I was skeptical because "Black people don't have emotional or mental issues," we just prayed about it, whatever "it" is and allowing the chips to fall where they may. I didn't realize I had fallen asleep until I felt my mother gently tapping on my shoulder, her way of saying she was leaving for work. Still in a daze, I rubbed my weary, dry eyes and wished my mother a great day. Following Dodie back into the house, we parted ways as we reached the living room, with Dodie heading to her car in the garage while I made my way to the bathroom.

The doorbell rang just as I finished getting dressed. Checking the time on my phone as I walked to the door, I like that the driver is punctual, might as well get it over with. Walking outside and shutting the door behind her, the driver waited patiently as I locked the door, escorting me to a waiting black Lincoln Navigator before opening the rear passenger door for me. We rode in silence as the sleek vehicle merged onto I-45 south towards Downtown before the driver finally spoke "Pardon me Ms. Gafford, do you have a music preference?"

"Boney James, if you have it."

"Yes ma'am"

As the intro to James' soulful "Sara Smile" began to fill the spacious SUV, I felt the tension ease just slightly, music had always been my safe place, allowing me to close my eyes throughout the rest of the ride. Roughly 15 minutes later we arrived at the destination, thanks in part to unusually light traffic in Houston's typically bustling downtown area. Normally I loved being downtown, but today was just another reminder of yet another thing that I couldn't enjoy with Colin anymore. The two of them used to come downtown for all kinds of reasons, any reason really, just to be downtown. Every city's residents brag about its beauty or skylines but being born and raised in Houston had instilled a sense of pride only true Houstonians understand. There was no city more beautiful than this one. But on that day, everything looked and felt different, a feeling I wasn't sure I would ever shake.

After I got out of the SUV, I took a minute to compose myself and then entered the building. After scanning the building directory, I made my way to the office I was scheduled to be in.

I walked into the office and informed the receptionist that I had an appointment - declining the drink that she offered in favor of getting started. I was already ready to go. A few moments later her phone buzzed, causing the receptionist to rise and instruct me to follow her as she led me to the doctor's office. Dr. Maurice Terry was an attractive man, he is about 6'0" tall about 180-190 lbs. His skin complexion was like roasted pecans his hair was immaculately cut which merged into a very neatly groomed beard and mustache, which made me self-conscious about my appearance. Today I was definitely eligible for winning first place for the "crawl under a rock and hide" look.

It's astonishing what can snap you back into the reality of life. With a probing gaze and the warmest light brown eyes, he looked as if he were looking through me, but oddly not in an intrusive way. It was if he could see the inner me that I'd carefully been hiding from the world. I felt naked. Walking over to me, Dr. Terry closed his office door and gently took both of my hands into his. Standing directly in front me he bowed his head as I stood silently, starting at him. To be honest I was slightly weirded out by what was going on. Then he began to pray, causing my body to stiffen as I froze in place. I absolutely was unprepared for this - I hadn't even prayed in months - it was an unnerving moment where I literally felt torn. Part of me felt a giant weight was being lifting away, but another part was fighting to ignore what was happening. What he was doing. It felt like my spirit was broken and dehydrated; he was trying to give me water and I was refusing it. Finally, I heard Dr. Terry say "amen." Opening his eyes, he found me staring at him curiously.

Dr. Terry offered me a seat, which I accepted. We sat in silence for a moment while I noticed he didn't have a notepad like the therapists on TV do. After a minute passed, he began with a quite simple, but probing, question.

"Why are you here?"

"I was sent here by Glenn Patterson."

"You didn't have to accept. So why are you here?"

I raised my eyebrow at him, wondering just what kind of little game he had going on, countering with "What kind of question is that Dr. Terry?"

"Call me Maurice; it's a simple question Victoria."

"I believe I've answered it."

"What happened on May 27, 1982?"

Caught off guard, I smiled slightly.

"I was born."

"What took place on January 25, 2004?"

My smile dissipated and my countenance shifted.

"I died."

"Okay, let's explore this response. Will you elaborate?"

"My son died, is that what you want to hear?!"

"What would you like to hear?"

Finally, I paused. I didn't know how to respond to the question. I sat for a few moments, my mouth moving silently as I struggled to respond but no words came out. There were a few different ways I could answer the question, but I settled on the one that made the most sense to me. The thing that I wanted the most.

"I want to hear that this has all been a horribly bad nightmare, or that I'm just stuck in a coma I can't wake up from. I want to hear Colin's voice again. I want someone to tell me that he'll be home when I get there. I want…"

By now the tears were flowing from my eyes, prompting Dr. Terry to hand me a box of tissue from his desk. He cleared his throat then asked me, "Victoria, why are you so angry?"

I hesitated. I tried to speak and then I closed my mouth again unsure if I was ready to face my demons. I lowered my gaze to stare at my intertwined hands, cleared my throat and the words started to flow freely...

"It was Super Bowl XXXVIII weekend when I buried my son…"

While most Houstonians were turned up and celebrating Super Bowl weekend, I was going through the absolute worst experience of my life; learning the hard way just how self-centered and self-absorbed some people can be. After the pretty speeches, all the flowers and the hollow promises, once the funeral was over the family had returned to my mother's house following the repast at the church. After that, it was over for everyone else. I didn't see it that way, because it was only the beginning of my own personal hell.

Meanwhile, my cousins just wanted me to use my connections - which could get them into virtually any party in the city that weekend - and all I wanted to do was fade into nonexistence. I entered my room and began to undress, staring at the reflection that looked back at me from the full-length mirror across the room. Starting at the crown of my head, my gaze then traveled down my face, staring directly at my eyes that were puffy, red, and dry. The moisture forming began to burn my eyes. My gaze continued further, coming to a stop at my breasts and midsection. For years I was a firm A cup but, thanks to Colin, I was now a full C cup. I looked at my waist, which wasn't as flat as it had once been, but portrayed no visible bulge either. There were no stretch marks, a fate I somehow escaped despite how large my stomach had grown while pregnant. Now, there was no visible physical evidence that I had ever been pregnant, a thought I bitterly pushed away as I wondered whether I was even fit to be someone's mother. I reached for my phone, dialing a number I told myself to avoid. I tried not to make this call often, yet here I am, becoming more and more dependent on drank. It helped ease the pain. I assumed that my mother considered me a full-blown alcoholic, but in reality, syrup was my drug of choice. When Eric first introduced me to it, I would do cute things like put jolly ranchers into my cup, gingerly watching them slip under the ice and to the bottom of the cup. After I became pregnant with Colin I quit completely, but with Colin gone… Tonight I didn't want to be cute; I wanted my drink "muddy," a mixture of cough syrup and sprite that would render me incoherent, allowing me to sleep virtually my life away. The phone only rang once before a familiar voice came onto the line. I placed my order with ease. Hanging up the phone, I tried to quickly think of a way to leave the house unnoticed without allowing my cousins to tag-along for the ride. But of course, my car was blocked in, making it impossible to leave without alerting at least one of my inquisitive, opportunistic family members. All the keys were in the living room, sitting uselessly as their owners talked and lingered behind. I wondered when they would finally leave. As I picked up my phone to make other arrangements, I looked up, unbeknownst to me; Tonya had entered the room and had been talking to me for nearly five minutes as I stared blankly. Now she stood, staring at me curiously.

"So, you're just going to be rude?"

Startled, I dismissively asked "What are you talking about?"

"I said, you haven't eaten all day and you need to eat something."

"I'm not hungry."

"I'm not leaving until you get something to eat."

I rolled my eyes and released a heavy sigh.

"There's plenty of food in the kitchen, I'll get something in a few minutes. Can you get Monica's keys and move her car so I can get out?"

"Why?"

What in the hell?! I was amazed that I was old enough to bury my son by myself but when I need people to move their vehicles, I had to pass an inquisition. There was no way to keep my secret a secret anymore and at this point I no longer even cared. Not caring was starting to become my mantra for life. "Ugh, fine! I have to run an errand."

"Dodie doesn't want you to be left alone…"

Now Vee was officially irritated.

"Look got damn it, I'm walking out of the door now. If you're coming then come on, if not then get out of my way and Give me your keys."

Backing out of the driveway, I decided to take the long way, taking the entrance ramp to I-45 North, and merging onto 610 East I made my way towards Fifth Ward. By the time we exited the freeway I couldn't tolerate Tonya's music selections any longer. Switching on the radio, Slim Thug's "3 Kings" instantly caught my ear; I would listen to any song that T.I. was featured on. Once I turned onto Liberty Rd, I called "Dough" to let him know that I was pulling up. I was pseudo bourgeoisie. I didn't mind driving to the hood to buy drank but wouldn't dare get out of my car and actually walk into the trap house to make the transaction. Dough would either deliver it to my location or I would pick it up curbside like a drive thru. I had never purchased this much at one time, but now that the funeral was over, my spending money had increased since it was just me to take care of, again. As I left Dough's spot, I felt my mood begin to shift. With my package now secured, I stopped by Hank's Seafood to grab something to eat. A well-known eatery, Hank's was bustling as the delicious smell of things like catfish filled the air around the small restaurant. Tonya had become unusually quiet, saying little other than a brief hushed phone conversation and a few sporadic texts. As we waited for our food at the drive-thru window, the other shoe dropped...

"So, are you feeling up to hanging out tonight?"

"Not at all…"

"You would feel better if you got out of the house, like what is sitting in the house supposed to accomplish? You need to get back to life."

Suddenly my appetite was gone. I didn't even wait on the food, instead I drove away from the restaurant and headed directly back to Studewood. Cousin or not, I wanted to slap the complete shit out of Tonya or better yet, put her out of the vehicle, however I settled for taking her back to my mother's house and locking myself inside of my room. The audacity of this bitch. I couldn't believe that Tonya had the nerve to say that, yet here we were. Once we were back at my mother's house, I gathered my belongings off the back seat and retreated to my bedroom, promptly locking the door. Grabbing a two liter of Sprite from the back of the closet, I removed the seal from a bottle of promethazine and emptied the entire bottle in the waiting soda. It had just become the most expensive bottle of Sprite I'd ever consumed. Gently rotating the bottle to ensure the concoction had thoroughly mixed I poured myself a cup and turned on the stereo - filling the air with Outkast's smooth "I Like the Way" before I switched to a throwback CD from the Port Arthur duo UGK, "Riding Dirty" In that moment as "One day" began to play, I fully understood the movement that Houston legend DJ Screw had started with the infectious, slow-banging sound now known globally as Screw music. As the music moved through me, I made a mental note to pick up a few Screw cd's the next day, as the tears began to fall. A few hours passed before I heard a soft knock on my door. It was Tonya, asking if I would accompany her to drop her sister-in-law off. I knew I was under the influence but decided to go since the trip from Studewood to Trinity Gardens was only 15 minutes, on a bad day. Leaving the house with Tonya, I settled into the backseat of the Expedition.

As we rode in silence, I didn't realize my eyes had drifted shut until I was suddenly startled by the biting sound of car horns blaring. After looking around and finally becoming aware of where I was, I instantly became irritated. Not only were we not in Trinity Gardens, but we were also on the other side of town on the Richmond strip - a Galleria area street home to numerous clubs and flashy cars whose owners often begged to be seen. The SUV soon came to a crawl as we entered gridlocked traffic, courtesy of the ongoing Super Bowl festivities. Any other time I would have loved to see my city so alive and full of activities; but right now, I couldn't enjoy it. I was dead inside. We sat in uncomfortable silence as I wondered where they were headed before Tonya veered into a packed, yet familiar, parking lot.

"Vee! Come on girl, let's go in here. I know you can get us in," Tonya half-joked as she pulled the car to a stop. "Y'all can go, I'll stay in the truck. I'm not going in there. Pointing to the slightly crushed sky-blue velour tracksuit she still had on from earlier I protested, "Even if I wanted to, I'm not dressed to go anywhere, Yet alone in there."

"You look fine" Tonya insisted. Shifting her tone, she added, "You know we can't get in without you, so are you going to stop moping and get us in, or what?"

Staring at them both incredulously, I responded by raising an eyebrow. I finally relented, telling them "Ok, stay here and I'll go see who's at the door." I got out of the truck and began to walk towards the front, but as soon as I was out of their view, I pulled out her phone, furiously typing in the number of Justin Broussard a longtime friend. He answered on the first ring.

"Hey Vee, is everything ok? Do you need anything?"

"Hey Justin, are you busy?"

"Never too busy for you, what's up?"

"I need a ride. Will you come get me?"

"Of course, where are you?"

After giving him my location, instead of heading back to the car I decided to wait inside of the Dave & Buster's restaurant next door. Let them find someone else to get them in. Right on cue, my phone began blowing up with calls from Tonya. I ignored everyone. If I would have been sober, I probably would have attacked Tonya by punching her right in her smug face for the continuous disrespect. Justin didn't take too long; as he was pulling up, I hurried into the passenger seat. I felt bad for calling him away from a night of fun and even though he kept telling me he didn't mind; I didn't like feeling that I was infringing on other people.

Hours later, I woke up in a daze. Jumping up startled, I didn't realize just how long I'd slept. I was fully dressed, thankfully, but I did not recognize my surroundings. Feeling panicked, Justin walked into the room with towels and an array of toiletries. He smiled at me, making my panic fade as my heartbeat settled back into a normal beat.

"Good Morning" I said. A half smile slowly forming on my lips.

"Good morning. It didn't seem right to take you home so late, so I brought you to my house instead. I hope that's ok?" Justin asked.

"It's fine."

"Good, now go get yourself together and meet me downstairs. Today it's all about you."

Now beaming, I could only smile in response. As the water from the shower cascaded over me, the heat and steam instantly made me feel better. After a long shower I finally exited, toweled off, wrapped myself in the soft cotton towel provided and looked at my reflection in the mirror. The flashback of thoughts back to when I first met Justin. It was the summer before I met Eric. I was having lunch with Dodie at Fuddruckers, my mother's favorite place for burgers. I was filling our cups with soda when Justin approached me.

"Good afternoon, what are you and your sister doing when y'all leave here?" I rolled my eyes, throwing back "You know damn well, that's not my sister," as I walked away.

Still, he persisted, following me to our table. As I sat back down, I held my breath and waited for the show that I knew was about to take place. Dodie was a woman that always spoke her mind. Always. And when it came to "pissy tailed li'l boys" - as she called them - chasing after her youngest daughter, she didn't play at all. Shoving his hand out to Dodie, Justin exclaimed "Good afternoon ma'am, your daughter just told me that you're her mother, not her sister, and I couldn't believe it. I had to come and tell you how beautiful you both are."

My mouth dropped. I'd never witnessed a guy be so bold with my mother, that was one of the main reasons that I hadn't bothered asking for permission to "talk to" a particular boy at school or otherwise. Dodie taught me that if a guy wasn't willing or too shy to meet my parents then he wasn't worth my time or attention. I always thought my mommy only said that to just deter me from boys completely, so Dodie's response surprised me even more. Firmly shaking Justin's hand, she replied, "Thank you, young man, what's your name?"

"Justin Broussard."

"Nice to meet you Justin, my name is Victoria, which is also my daughter's name." Turning and looking directly at me she said, "Now this is the type of young man you should be dating."

I sat in silence, stunned. My mother had never approved of me dating due to my age and the fact that she just didn't like the guys that I chose to talk to. Even though I tried to explain to her that I wasn't seriously entertaining any of the guys. How else was I supposed to learn how to deal with the opposite sex if I never had any type of interaction? Justin continued to smile as he asked me for my pager number. I provided him with the information he requested, along with my home phone number. Considering I already had my mother's approval - which was a miracle in itself - I figured he must be a good catch. But roughly a few months later I would learn another life lesson: Everything that glitters is not gold. Pretty soon we were officially dating; unbeknownst to me our relationship was only exclusive on my side. My first relationship life lesson came sooner than expected as we made our way to the Ice Breakers step show for Black Greek organizations. It was our first official date as a couple.

Despite being a freshman in college, Justin didn't mind that I was still in high school. It was the summer before my senior year and I was experiencing my first taste of freedom, something I'd been allowed to enjoy that night thanks to a simple request from Justin and of course some begging to Dodie for permission to attend. After an amazing show, we made our way to Justin's car, pausing as a group of his friends called out his name. Handing me the car keys, he told me he'd join me shortly. With a kiss on the cheek and a hand smack on my derrière, I continued towards the car without him, picking up the pace as the parked car came into view. I climbed inside and waited for Justin, the minutes crawling by slowly as I started to become impatient. 15 minutes later, Justin still hadn't joined me, and I was tired of waiting. I decided to take matters into my own hands; deftly sliding over into the driver's seat and starting the car with the intention of finding Justin. I started with the parking lot, driving around it while scanning the sea of faces still entering and exiting the auditorium. I reached over and turned the radio back up, allowing my jam "Notorious Thugs" to pour through the speakers as I, although irritated, searched for

Justin's face. As I turned to circle back around again my eyes suddenly locked in on Justin - who was neither with the friends he'd left with, nor alone - with a young woman that handed him back his phone with a knowing smile. Adding insult to injury, she blew Justin a kiss before walking away, incensing my irritation to anger even more. I was livid, throwing my anger into pounding the car horn in front of me in an effort to get Justin's attention. With the surrounding vehicles causing the same, if not more of the same amount of noise, it took a few moments for Justin to register that the sound he was hearing was coming from his own car. Staring into the headlights his eyes narrowed as he finally recognized it was me behind the steering wheel, my face contorted in anger, the horn still blaring as I continued to push, push, and push. Jogging over, Justin calmly opened the car door, switching places with me as I, seething asked "Who is she?!" Not missing a beat, he answered, "Just some girl whose number my little cousin wanted. He was too scared to talk to her, so I helped him out. He's fam."

"So why did she blow you a kiss?"

"She didn't blow me a kiss."

"Oh ok."

And with that I was done, buckling my seatbelt, I sat mutely, staring out the passenger side window. 'So, this is what heartbreak feels like' I thought. This was weird for me; I didn't fully know how to process it. All I knew was that I no longer wanted to be near Justin, let alone in a car with him. When he asked me what I wanted to eat, I told him to take me home.

"Why?"

"I don't feel good, my stomach is cramping."

Cramps will get a woman out of practically any situation, a tactic I learned shortly after beginning the menstrual stage of life and that I leaned on to end a perfect night that had gone to shit. I wouldn't speak to Justin for months after that. I'm sure he thought I was immature for ghosting him, but I didn't care. I felt like he was immature for lying to my face. For a long while Dodie would ask about him from time to time, but after I began dating Eric, she stopped asking about Justin. And that was that.

But life goes on. Eventually we would become great friends, able to laugh at the memory of our young, failed romance. Now, I couldn't help but wonder what the future might hold, my thoughts interrupted by the smell of bacon wafting from the kitchen. My stomach began to do somersaults as I followed my nose to the kitchen. Justin had shocked me, preparing a full breakfast that included French toast, fruit, bacon, sausage, eggs and one my favorites, and grits with cheese. We spoke little while eating, simply enjoying one another's company before Justin asked whether I had any plans for the day. I didn't. After calling my mother to let her know that I was safe, which was not a simple task at all...

"Victoria! Where are you? I've been worried..."

"I apologize mommy. I'm ok, there's no need to be worried."

"Tonya called me saying that you left them somewhere and they were worried that something happened to you."

"Mommy, no they weren't. They wanted to go out and I didn't, so I called a ride and left so they could continue their fun. We can finish this conversation when I get home." After I hung up the phone, Justin suggested we leave, taking me to the Galleria mall for a little retail therapy. I soon realized that the day was just getting started as Justin took me to the spa after our shopping trip, pampering me with a massage along with a manicure and pedicure. All things I needed badly. I was grateful and happy; it was the most relaxed I felt in a long time. After the spa, we went back to Justin's home to drop off the bags and get dressed for dinner with his friends. For the first time in a long time, I was able to let go and relax, the drinks flowing through dinner and beyond as I held my own, shot for shot.

Eventually, the night escaped me...

There was blackness. We often think of what we'd do in a given situation, hopeful that our more rational side will prevail against whatever we may face. But sexual assault comes in various forms, including acts committed by acquaintances, friends and even family members. In this case I knew exactly what was happening when I woke up with Justin on top of me. Feeling woozy, I screamed the word "NO!" repeatedly, begging him to stop as he pulled my arms above my head and continued before I blacked out again. Even though I was fully aware of what date rape was, I couldn't, wouldn't bring myself to say the words out loud. That little bit of hope? The butterflies that had been floating in my stomach whenever Justin was nearby? Gone. It was all gone. Very much in control of the situation, when it was over, he drove me to my cousin's house as if nothing had happened. Confident that his vile actions would go unreported and unfortunately, thanks to my fear - and shame - he was right. It was as if he were oblivious to the piece of me, he'd just ripped away. Or perhaps he just didn't care.

****

"If you're going to be a slut and a whore you need to go somewhere else and do that!"

Tonya stated in a matter-of-fact tone of voice.

It was her way of greeting me as I walked through her door.

My blood began to boil. But still, I couldn't bring myself to tell her, to scream out, what had happened to me. I couldn't urge myself to go through a rape kit, an interrogation and I damn sure could not coerce myself to write the word 'rape' down on paper. That would make it real. This wasn't some guy with a creepy van, or the pervert from up the street. Society has all the answers about avoiding the deviants of the world, except when that deviant turns out to be someone that you know and trust. It was too raw and too personal - and I just couldn't bring myself to share it with anyone. And definitely not with Tonya. Instead, I left, gathering my things as hot tears threatened to spill onto the carpeted floor. Life wasn't done with me yet, but I had reached my limit with life. Acute Stress Disorder/PTSD is what professionals would suggest I was unknowingly suffering from; I was a ticking time-bomb just waiting to explode. Unchecked and untreated because "Black families don't have mental illness." But as I was quickly learning, not everything can be "prayed away." I should have been in counseling, right after Colin died, not-self-medicating. Soon, I'd find myself holding a bottle of pills. Another soul allowed to silently slip through the cracks. Another one...

"You have my sincerest condolences." It was a phrase that I remembered all too well. In the days, and months, after the tragic accident - it was all I'd heard. Usually, whispered to me very quietly before the speaker awkwardly pulled me in for an embrace. It wasn't their fault. They meant well, but few knew the right words for this type of situation. Your child is supposed to bury you, not the other way around. It was an experience that I wouldn't wish on even my worst enemy. After reading the card again I put it away, making a mental note to thank the sender for their condolences. I appreciated the sentiment, even though it did nothing to stop the pain. After the dead are buried, life continues to go on. A bitter pill that I was tired of swallowing, I was tired... so utterly tired. For the last week I'd spent my time inside of a bottle, using the dark liquid to take the edge off of the biting grief I'd slowly grown accustomed to living with. The house was dark and, for now, quiet. Alone with my thoughts, guilt consumed me – mentally agonizing over and over the "what ifs" …

What if I would've just taken Colin to church with me?

What if I would've just stayed at home?

What if Eric and I had never broken up?

What if I never gave birth…

knowing what awaited me that day - I'd carefully shut myself off from the world. Tying up any loose ends without arousing suspicion in my family and friends. I knew that they cared, but even their love wasn't enough to pull me out of the hole I'd fallen into. Nothing mattered anymore, because at the other side of it all there was someone waiting for me.

My baby. For years I'd gone through life with the short end of the stick, trailed by a string of bad luck that somehow, I'd always overcome, despite the emotional toll involved. This time was different, however. My only begotten son was gone, a shock and blow that even my strong will couldn't absorb. On days when the liquor won, I would stumble through the house in a stupor. Drifting into the bedroom right next to my own, I would sit for hours inhaling the last scents of the child I'd never hold again. It was one of those days. Choking back a sob, I sank into the carpet, my eyes growing heavy as the pills I'd chased with whiskey began to go into effect. I knew that it was time; soon, I would see my son again. Before I lost consciousness, a familiar voice rang throughout my head: "Mommy, please don't leave!" As I went under, I remembered the words, vowing to never leave his side again.

I only remember my eyes opening and I was in a dimly lit room. I realized quickly that I was in a hospital room and I tried to move but my body felt so heavy, and my head was feeling as if there was a marching band inside of it. I groaned in agony as I tried to adjust myself in the bed.

"Thank you, Father in Heaven."

I heard Dodie say softly. A single tear left my eye and trailed slowly down my cheek as I looked intently at her very worried face.

"I'm so sorry mommy."

"You have nothing to be sorry for, my baby. I'm just thankful you're still here with us. We'll talk later, let's get you some food."

Dodie held my hand and rubbed my head until the nurse came.

I sat there quietly, staring at the foot of the chair that held Dr. Terry. I had just unveiled my soul, exposing a secret I'd refused to accept, let alone share with anyone else: I was date raped a few days after I buried my only son. They were words I hadn't told another living person, choosing to throw it on the pile of burdens I was already tasked with carrying. When I finally looked up, I saw Dr. Terry staring directly into my eyes. And in his eyes, I saw horror, shock and pity staring back at me. A knowing look that I hated, especially the pity. It was a look that signaled, at least to me, that it was time to cut the session short. I got up to leave. After what seemed like an eternity passed, he finally spoke.

"What are your thoughts at this moment?"

"I'm ready to leave..."

"Victoria, you have a homework assignment."

"Homework?!"

"Yes, I want you to hug your mother for five minutes."

I looked at Dr. Terry as if he'd lost his damn mind. Hug my mother?? What was so significant about hugging my mother? This confirmed my opinion that counseling is a tremendous waste of time.

"Ok, Dr. Terry."

"See you next week Victoria."

"Bye Dr. Terry."

After the driver dropped me back off at home, I immediately entered the house in search of Dodie.

I found her in the kitchen, a familiar hum echoing throughout the room as she cooked in peace. Her back was facing me as I gave her a brief hug. Instantly her hands stopped chopping vegetables, wiping them on her apron as she turned around and pulled me in closer for another hug. A proper one. I could feel my emotions clawing to the surface as I buried my face in her embrace. I tried to pull away, but mommy wouldn't let go. As my eyes started to fill with tears, I struggled against her, causing her to hold me even tighter. A blood curdling scream escaped my lips as I collapsed into sobs, crying until I was too weak to stand. I cried and cried, and still, my mommy never let go. Emotionally drained, after the tender moment with my mother, I retreated to my room, lying across the bed. Not wanting to be alone, yet not ready to breakdown in front of my mother again, I picked up the phone - calling Stacie to see if she was free to hang out later. I didn't want to stay at home, but I also didn't want to go out alone. Lately, all my "friends" seemed to be turning into enemies, at least in my eyes. I had always been complacent and passive in my friendships, allowing toxic friends to linger around due to their "history." Now, at the loneliest point in my life, I didn't have any friends, no longer had my man, and wasn't even sure if I could still call Jesus a friend. And so, I called Stacie, a girl I met at church. We had quite a bit in common. We both came from large families, both goal oriented and had similar personality styles. Stacie was free and we decided to go have dinner and drinks. Which was another thing we had in common, we were both foodies. We met up at Sam's Boat on Richmond. Stacie is a hilarious person; we share the same sarcastic sense of humor. Unlike myself however, Stacie doesn't drink alcohol. That was our first hang out together, but it wouldn't be our last. Stacie became my best friend. She is always brutally honest and never sugar coats anything. That's an extremely rare quality that I love about her.

No false pretense.

Chapter Three

"I can't believe this bitch! Who the fuck does she think she is?!" Eric slammed the phone down, not caring that he'd just cracked the base in half. He couldn't believe that Vee had just called him out the blue, after months had gone by, to inform him he was obligated to be at a fucking deposition in just two days. Classic Victoria.

"Didn't I tell you that I don't care about a fucking insurance claim? That stupid motherfucker didn't even get jail time!"

"It's beyond an insurance claim. It's a civil suit and you have to choose a side because the insurance company doesn't want any more lawsuits arising at a later date."

"Man, fuck you and that damn insurance company."

He could tell by her voice that she wasn't in the mood to play around. Cool yet calm, she responded "That's fine. Look you have two options: Either do the damn deposition, collect your check, and get the fuck out of my life...or I can have your name removed from Colin's death certificate and you won't get a damn thing. That shouldn't bother you at all since you never signed his birth certificate."

He took a deep breath, struggling to match her frigid demeanor he spat, "You are such an evil bitch."

"And you are a selfish ass bum."

"Text me the address. For-"

dial tone

Victoria

I still hadn't figured out how Dr. Maurice Terry circumvented my emotional barriers however, in this moment I was very thankful that he was in my life. After I hung up in Eric's face, I sent Maurice a text message urgently requesting for him to call me as soon as possible. Ninety agonizing minutes later, he did.

"So, I finally told Eric about the deposition."

"The same deposition that you're scheduled to be at in two days?"

The way Maurice said it, seemed like I was the one that was wrong in this situation.

"Yes, that's the only deposition that I'm going to."

"Victoria… You don't, on any level, expect me to believe that you don't see any error in your actions?"

"No, Maurice, I don't expect you to believe that. However, I attempted to inform Eric in the beginning. Eric acted as if his decision to be against the lawsuit was the final decision for the both of us. And typical of him, he didn't feel it was necessary to give me an explanation why. So, I decided to take matters into my own hands for once. Had Eric chose to at least respect me enough to explain his reasoning, I would've called Glenn and terminated everything before it even got this far."

"Tit for tat is not healthy for situations like this. Someone has to be the bigger person, Victoria."

"Why do I always have to be the bigger person? I'm only 5'5"

After our laughter subsided, Maurice continued.

"You can't continue to carry this enormous amount of anger. You have to do the work to get the results."

Eric

If looks could kill the malice in Eric's eyes would have done the job to everyone in that conference room, several times over. He didn't want to be there, and it showed, namely because he didn't understand why he even needed to be questioned about his son's death. He wasn't even there when it happened, which meant he had little to no details since he'd never wanted to know. However, during the criminal trial for the people that had killed his son, he gave a victim's impact statement in hopes that the judge would give the maximum sentence allowed. It didn't turn out that way. All that silly simple bitch of a judge did was what amounted to a slap on the wrist: 7 years' incarceration eligible for parole in 3 years. The defendants each had extensive prior criminal records and even though two witnesses came forward at the time, because the officer on the scene neglected to verify that the search warrant was accurate, all evidence collected linking them to the shooting was thrown out and the charges were lowered to felon in possession of a firearm for both defendants. They then pleaded out to the agreed upon terms. Justice served. Justice?! What about us the parents of the victim?!

"Mr. Spencer, we're ready to get started."

State your name, DOB, and address for the record please.

"Eric Marcus Spencer; April 10, 1980; 7518 Lavender St Houston, TX 77026."

When did you become a father?

"March 08, 1999"

Are you aware of the events that took place January 25, 2004?

"Somewhat."

Would you please give us your version of the events that took place that day?

"My son was murdered in a drive-by shooting."

Were you happy to be a father?

"Absolutely"

Why didn't you sign your son's birth certificate?

"I wasn't there when he was born."

Why weren't you present for the birth?

"His mother didn't call me until after he was born."

Do you know why that is so?

Eric glared at Victoria before responding.

"No"

Was there any uncertainty in regard to paternity?

"What the fu-" Eric released a harsh breath, adjusted himself in the seat, shook his head and answered seething.

"No, there wasn't any damn uncertainty in regard to paternity. Colin is… was my only son."

I understand Mr. Spencer. Let's move on.

What plans, if any, do you have for this amount of money you're pursuing?

"None."

Are you in serious debt?

"No."

Are you addicted to any illegal drugs?

"No."

Do you have a history of illegal drug use?

"No."

Do you have any other children?

"No."

Do you plan to have any more children?

"...No."

Are you acquainted with any of the defendants in this case?

"Man, Hel- No"

Eric tried to answer the questions, without yelling, to the best of his ability for the most part. He felt some of the questions were completely outlandish and ridiculous, still, it was nothing compared to listening to the answers that Victoria gave. As he watched her answer her own set of questions, Eric thought he would die right there in that room.

"State your name, DOB and address for the record please."

"Victoria Simone Gafford; May 27, 1982; 7518 Lavender street Houston, TX 77026"

When did you become a mother?

"The day I learned I was pregnant."

Were you happy to be a mother?

"Absolutely."

What was your son's name?

"Colin Sean Spencer."

Are you aware of the events that took place January 25, 2004?

"Yes."

Will you please recall, in as much detail as possible, your knowledge of the days before, during and after that date?

"What do the days before have to do with any of this?"

Glen Patterson objected on Victoria's behalf on the basis of relevance. The mediator asked the opposing counsel to explain the purpose of the question. We need to establish the mother's pattern of behavior.

The mediator looked at Victoria and stated, "Please answer the question."

With a heavy sigh Victoria started, "On the day before my son died, I was supposed to go on a date, but canceled at the last minute because Colin didn't want me to go. The following day I woke up late, so I was rushing to get dressed for work or church rather. After I finished getting Colin dressed, I sat him on the sofa next to my dad so that I could get dressed. After I was done, I went to get Colin and saw that my dad had allowed him to make a mess with his finger paint set, so I decided to leave him there while I went to church. My mom had already left me behind because I was late, so I decided to have my dad drop me off since my own car was blocked in. When we arrived at the church, I went to hug, and kiss Colin goodbye and he went bananas. He started screaming and crying to stay with me, but his clothes were so messed up that I didn't want to take him inside looking like that. So, I went inside and watched my dad drive away with Colin utterly upset. A short time later, I received a call on the church phone from my neighbor telling me to hurry home because there was an ambulance in front of my mother's home. My mother and I raced home and upon reaching the house I got out of the car and found my brother in the back of the ambulance. As I tried to enter the house, a detective blocked me from entering and then I saw the EMT's exiting the house with a small body completely covered. Then I passed out. When I regained consciousness, I awoke to my mother frantically trying in get in touch with Eric, Colin's father. He finally answered and met us at the hospital. Eric and I then had to sign paperwork in order to remove our son from life support. We stayed for a while after that, and then went our separate ways. The following morning, HPD homicide detectives rang the doorbell and requested to speak to me. I was informed that after dropping me off at church, my father, brother, and son were standing in the front yard, when suddenly a car came careening down the street. As the car approached our home, the occupants started shooting. My father fell to the ground and my brother grabbed my son and was struck in his arm as he tried to get into the house. The defendants then drove away from the scene. My brother didn't realize that the bullet had exited his arm and went into

Colin's head until long after the shooting stopped. The detectives then informed me that both the driver and the vehicle had been identified and were in the process of being located. As we were talking the doorbell rang again, it was a CPS representative; there to do a welfare check on any other children that I possibly had, a legal requirement in the death of any child apparently. I informed the rep that I didn't have any other children, nor did any children live in the house before promptly slamming the door in her face. That is my recollection of events in that time frame.

Do you plan to have any more children?

"No, I do not."

Are you, or were you acquainted with the defendant prior to this event?

"No."

Why are you requesting this amount of money?

"Because there's no such thing as an infinite amount."

What plans, if any, do you have for this amount of money?

"Whatever comes to my mind."

Are you in serious debt?

"No."

Are you addicted to illegal drugs?

"No."

Do you have a history of illegal drug use?

"No."

After they were done with their probing question and answer session, the insurance company's attorneys left the room, retreating to another one down the hall. For the next three hours notes would pass back and forth between the two rooms in an effort to determine just how much farther the proceedings would go. Finally, in the last 15 minutes of the reserved time period left for mediation, the insurance company made their final offer: $1.3 million dollars.

Mr. Patterson finally showed me the document that had been passed back and forth for the last three hours. Now, the ball was in my court to either accept with conditions or reject it completely and go to trial.

"What happens if we go to trial?"

"You could possibly get more money; however, the process would take longer, and you would have to repeat this entire process all over again, only in front of a judge and jury."

"What happens if I accept this offer?"

"You the parents would sign a nondisclosure agreement as

well as an agreement that this would end any future lawsuits or litigation for any and all reasons. My office would receive a check on your behalf in about 30-90 days. Shortly thereafter your checks will be released to you upon verification of a valid bank account. And that would be the end of this process."

I shook my head. This is what it all came down to, putting a price tag on a priceless part of myself. Reluctantly I decided...

"I'll accept the offer."

I instantly felt like I had just sold my soul by putting a dollar sign on the life of my precious baby boy.

Chapter Four

I don't know why I am speeding down Highway 288. Club Visions wasn't going anywhere, and I hated arriving at the club before midnight. Reaching for my Nextel, I called Stacie to let her know I was almost at her house. Hanging up the phone I quickly opened the visor mirror to scan my make-up and refresh my MAC lip glass. Flipping the visor back up I turned my signal light on to exit before being distracted by a man in a Chevrolet Avalanche waving his phone at me. As I lowered my tinted window to see what he wanted the driver started pointing at the exit, so I assumed he wanted to get over in front of me. Lucky for him I was in a great mood, so

I obliged him, watching as he navigated his truck in front of mine and towards the light at Old Spanish Trail. Once I reached the OST light, I turned into the gas station to fill up, paying no mind as the same Avalanche pulled up beside me while I finished pumping my gas. Now it was his turn to lower his window, allowing me to make contact with the most intense set of warm, darkly seductive eyes that I had ever seen.

"Good evening, Beautiful"

"Good evening."

"You look amazing, where are you headed tonight?" His eyes roamed from the top of my head and briefly down to the red, white, and black silk Jimmy Choo heels I had on.

"Out," I responded.

His smile disarmed me. I'd never met a man with such a beautiful smile, his teeth sparkling white and straight. Beaming wholeheartedly, I couldn't help but return the smile that eased onto my face.

"So... you're not as mean as you're trying so hard to be right now. I'd love to take you out; can I have your phone number?"

"I tell you what, you can give me yours and if I find some free time, I'll call you."

He laughed, "Ok. I look forward to hearing from you, and my name is Dominic since you didn't ask."

I just smiled. I had no intention of ever calling him, but it was fun just going through the motions again. The greeting experience was a warm welcome after shutting myself off from the world for what had been a tumultuous entire year.

I got back in my car and turned back onto OST to go pick up Stacie. Once she was in the car we peeled off into the night as I put my current favorite CD, Urban Legend, on.

"I don't know why you even bother to go out Vee, it's not like you're going to give any man that tries to talk to you the time of day."

"I didn't realize that it was a requirement to give a guy my number just because he buys a drink or tells me that I'm cute."

Stacie laughed, "No, but you should at least get one phone number and talk to somebody. Go on one date. It's ok to get back into the dating scene now."

"For your information, I just acquired a gentleman's phone number at the gas station before I picked you up... na na na boo boo" I teased, sticking my tongue out at her for an added effect.

Laughing, "It doesn't matter since we both know you're not going to call him." Stacie jokingly rolled her eyes and turned the music back up.

The girl's night out with Stacie was just what I needed, but in the weeks that followed I buried myself in work. Up until Colin's death I'd always maintained certain boundaries regarding my musical gift, only accepting church bookings with exceptions made for funerals and weddings. But lately I've been taking whatever came my way, as long as it included a check or cash payment. Today I was lending my gift to a local music producer named Key Tones. Prior to today I'd never heard of him, which went without saying because he wasn't a part of the church circuit, but he'd been referred by a mutual friend that just didn't have the heart to tell Key Tones that he didn't have the creativity needed to succeed as a producer. I didn't care about his creativity, or lack of. Nor did I care about how he chose to waste his time or money. All I cared about was the fact that he'd paid for an entire day of work - in cash - requesting only an hour of my time in return. The easiest money I had ever made, it was something I could see myself doing long-term. True to his word, roughly an hour later I was already walking out of the building after laying the tracks. Done for the day, I called Stacie - who'd grown to become my best friend - to see if she was free for lunch. To my great disappointment she wasn't, anxiety rising as I scrambled to find something to fill my time. I hadn't returned to a point emotionally or mentally, where I could be alone for an extended period of time. I was trying, but it was still a process. Now I had three hours before my mother would be home from work and no one else to call. Then I remembered the man I met at the gas station. I couldn't remember his name, but I had time, spending the next 20 minutes doing a line-by-line search through the contact list in my phone for a name I did not recognize. Finally, I came across a weird name - crossing my fingers I pressed the call button and hoped for the best. I also made a mental note to do some much-needed deletions later that day.

"Hello beautiful."

"Do you call every woman you talk to, beautiful?"

"No."

"Then how do you know I'm beautiful?"

"I remember your face."

"Do you know who you're speaking with?"

"Yes."

"Oh,really?"

"Absolutely."

"What's my name?"

"You didn't tell me your name."

"So how do you know who you're talking to?"

"Your number isn't saved in my phone so it can't be anyone else" the voice answered in a matter-of-fact tone, prompting me to laugh.

"My name is Vee" I said with a smile.

"What are your plans for today; would you allow me the pleasure of seeing you again?"

I paused, "Sure, where would you like to meet?"

"Let's meet at the Pappadeaux's on 610."

"Ok, what's a good time for you?"

"1:30."

"I'll be there, promptly at that time."

As always, I arrived on time, pulling into a parking spot I called Dominic to see where he was.

"Hey Beautiful"

"Are you here?"

"I'm 5 minutes away."

"So, you'll be here at 1:35p?"

"Yes, absolutely"

"Ok, if you're not, I'm leaving."

Dominic laughed, amused by Victoria's insistence on punctuality.

I meant what I said. After waiting another five minutes he still hadn't arrived, so I left the restaurant and headed home. He had no clue who he was dealing with. By 1:45pm my phone was ringing, and I had a fairly good idea of who it was. I chuckled as Dominic's name continued to light up on the screen. Surprising myself, I answered the call.

"Hello."

"Where are you, beautiful?"

"In my car."

"Come inside, I'm walking in."

"I left at 1:35"

Vee could hear the smile in his tone as he asked, "You left?"

"Yes."

"Ok beautiful, maybe some other time then."

"Yeah, maybe."

Dominic

Dominic found himself staring at the phone, amused, and briefly shocked as a smile warmed his face. He wasn't accustomed to women brushing him off. At all. He'd dated scores of beautiful women, but he noticed that most had low self-esteem and required some type of male validation. This one was different. Vee was beautiful, and she knew it. More importantly, it seemed as if she had her head on straight. At first, he planned on just smashing and dashing, because she was much younger, and typically women her age were flighty - always on the hunt for someone that could benefit them financially. He couldn't quite put his finger on it, but Vee was different. He didn't know how, but he'd already decided to make it his mission to find out. Driving away from the restaurant, Dominic headed to Smitty's, a sports bar he owned in 3rd Ward. He rarely made an appearance there, mostly because he didn't want to be publicly affiliated with any of his businesses. But this was an important meeting with his supplier. By his calculations, the meeting would be done, and he would be gone long before the bar opened. The grind never stopped, and Dominic had goals that could not be deterred, and right now that included making sure that the bricks of cocaine, he oversaw kept his other business ventures running smoothly. He was proud of how far he'd come in life, but he wasn't proud of some of things he'd had to do to get there - things he reasoned that were the necessary evils that came with the dealer lifestyle. The game was the game. He'd taken risks that, if caught, would have cost him his life or freedom, but he had no regrets whatsoever.

Victoria

When the phone rang, I didn't recognize the number that appeared on the screen, reluctantly answering it in hopes it was a potential client. It wasn't. At the other end of the line was a representative from a company known as Life Gift. Apparently, in the shuffle of paperwork I had signed at the hospital, I'd inadvertently given authorization for Colin's organs to be given to someone in need. Now, the representative was calling to inform me that their annual gala and awards ceremony was approaching, and Colin was going to be honored for his contribution.

"I understand Ms. Gafford that this call has blindsided you and I sincerely apologize for this, but if possible, I would love to be able to confirm your attendance."

"Will you please give me some time to think about this? Is there a number that I can call back once I make a decision?"

"Absolutely, you can reach me directly at 713-523-4428. And take your time; we don't need confirmation until 2 weeks from today. Please have a wonderful day."

I was torn. On one hand, a piece of my baby was still alive and functioning, courtesy of the organ he'd donated; and I would have the opportunity to meet the recipient if I chose to do so. Still, part of me couldn't help but be somewhat angry, and bitter, that pieces of my son were flourishing inside of someone else instead of inside of Colin's body. Because Colin isn't here anymore. Worse still, I couldn't help but feel as if my DNA was now residing inside of a complete stranger. Sensing where my mind was headed, I snatched open my phone and pressed the button to quick dial a priority contact.

Dr. Terry answered on the second ring. He was glad that I called. Ever since our first meeting, he'd told me that something in his spirit had told him that I needed more than the typical doctor/patient interaction; and slowly but surely, we were making progress with healing. albeit everything had to be on my terms. However, once I opened a door, he always took advantage to push me thru it, figuratively.

"I need to meet with you, ASAP…"

"Hey, what's wrong? I have some extra time after lunch. Want to meet at a restaurant or would you rather come to the office?" He could hear the pain in my voice.

"I'll come to the office when you get done with lunch, I'm not hungry."

It was yet another example of why Maurice was so drawn to Victoria in such a protective manner. Not only was she brave but the strength she exuded is so effortless. In all his years of practice, he'd never met a young woman quite like her. He'd become a therapist to help people, however with Victoria he slipped into a protective big brother role. He knew from the day he met her that God had allowed their paths to cross for the very reason that she needed protection more than she ever cared to admit. Because of this he made sure to pick up some food for the both of them. He finished arranging it as Vee walked into his office with frustration written all over her face. She paused when she saw what he had done, her lips curving into a slight smirk.

"Hey Victoria, what's bothering you?"

"I received a call from a non-profit organization today. Life Gift. It was brought to my attention that when I signed the paperwork in the hospital during Colin's...situation...I gave authorization for his organs to be donated."

Vee began to cry.

"Here, have a seat and try to eat something. Take a minute to breathe and then we'll talk."

Victoria did just that, taking a couple bites of the pasta that he had bought, followed by a few sips of ice-cold water. She knew that it was a stall tactic, allowing Dr. Terry to essentially kill two birds with one stone, getting Vee to eat while also giving her a minute to compose herself before they talked - his way of helping her learn to control her emotions and still be logical at the same time.

Once she finished bringing him up to speed about the phone call, Vee waited slightly impatiently for Dr. Terry to give her advice. And as usual, he subtly helped pushed her to think the situation out herself before settling on a conclusion that would work best for her. As smart as she was, Vee still hadn't figured out what his ultimate end-goal was: to get her confidence and self-assurance back up to 100%. What most people don't realize, those closely impacted by a death, and especially a young mother like Victoria, is that the death of a child can create a shift for those left behind. For Vee, her paradigm shifted not once but twice. The first being the shift into motherhood, and the second in figuring out how to redirect her mothering energy into a healthy direction, now that she was no longer a mother in the physical sense - the latter being the most difficult, a hurdle that caused most to self-destruct.

In the end, I decided to attend the gala. I didn't have a specific reason for going, but I viewed it the same way I had viewed Colin's funeral arrangements. It was just something that had to be done.

So, I went.

Nestled inside of Downtown Houston, the Magnolia Hotel is incredibly beautiful, giving it a well-earned reputation for its style and decor. Trying to steady my nerves, I admired the ambiance as I walked around the massive lobby. Scanning the directory, I quickly located the ballroom for the Life Gift banquet. I'd challenged myself to brave the event alone, a decision I was swiftly starting to regret as anxiety began to taunt me. I stopped at the hotel's bar, ordered a warmed shot of Gentleman Jack to soothe my rattled nerves. Downing the shot in one smooth gulp, I said a quick prayer to God for additional strength and finally proceeded to the ballroom. Thankfully, the ceremony was neither long nor drawn out, in fact, I grudgingly admitted, that it was rather nice - the donor and recipient introductions were both endearing and heartwarming. Not all of the donors were deceased; however, some were alive to meet the people that had graciously accepted their invaluable donation. A fact I couldn't help but notice as I struggled to check the bitterness that still simmered inside of me now and then. As Colin's name was called, the emcee recited his brief bio and history, giving me a humongous sense of pride that my baby was the center of attention, although brief, as they celebrated him after death. The recipient was a beautiful little girl roughly his age, and though I was still in pain, I couldn't help but feel amazed that this precious child has had and would continue to have a new opportunity at life because of my son's sacrifice. Lost in my own thoughts, I was shocked when my own name was called. It was a moment of truth for me, as I had to immediately decide if I would walk onto the stage to meet the recipient and receive the plaque on my son's behalf, or if I would remain frozen in my seat. Every fiber in my soul begged me to remain seated, but something more powerful than myself compelled me to rise. Pulling myself to my feet, I walked to the front with confidence that belied the belly of terror and trepidation I truly felt. Forcing myself up the stairs and onto the stage, as I accepted the heavy plaque from the presenter, I was momentarily knocked off balance by a small force that had wrapped itself around my legs. Looking down all I saw was a puff ball of hair and a pair of small arms hugging my legs tightly, much like Colin used to do. Then, an older woman made her way on stage, apologizing profusely as she tried to pry her child from around my legs. I tried to assure the woman, who looked both ashamed and mortified, "That's not necessary, no apology needed."

Our unlikely trio moved to the far side of the stage as I finally unwrapped the child from around me. Kneeling down so that we could be face to face, I became lost in the biggest, prettiest hazel brown eyes I'd ever seen.

"What is your name, sweetie?"

"Shailene," she whispered with a smile. Her bright eyes opening even wider as she stared at me in wonder and amazement.

"Hello Shailene, I'm Victoria… it's wonderful to meet you." Despite the smile plastered across my face, my eyes - now on the brink of overflowing - betrayed me. Still, I extended my hand to the little girl, who looked at my outstretched hand and then flung herself into my chest. Wrapping her small arms tightly around my neck. I was stunned. Suddenly, I could not move. Then, Shailene's small voice made its way to my ear.

"Thank you," she whispered coyly. Her voice sweet and pure.

Unable to hold my tears back any longer, my eyes began to flow as I embraced the girl in return. After what seemed like forever, I reluctantly released the little girl, giving her a final look before parting ways. I knew it was time to go. Leaving the event after our exchange, my heart was heavy, yet my shoulders were light at the same time; a huge part of me now elated that I had decided to go. Not knowing whether I would ever see the little girl again, I took solace in the fact that another child was alive because of my son. Because of Colin…

Victoria

March 8, 2005. My baby boy would have been six years old today, but instead of getting decorations ready for a birthday party; I'm at Houston Memorial Gardens placing flowers and toy trucks on his grave. Back in January I'd tried to visit his grave, but it was just too much for me. I was borderline hysterical before I could even drag myself out of the house. Today my eyes are misty, but I'm here. I made it. I was so caught up in the moment that I didn't hear the car drive up and park, nor did I hear the footsteps that approached behind me. I didn't realize I wasn't alone there, until I felt a strong pair of arms wrap around me. I didn't have to turn around to know who they belonged to; Eric was here.

In that moment, all of the bottled-up pain and hurt bubbled up from inside of me, finally escaping my mouth as I sobbed in agony. We haven't spoken with nor seen each other in over a year and we didn't speak to each other then. Instead, we just stood there not facing one another, silent, neither one of us wanting to ruin a moment of semi-normalcy. Though our son was buried in the ground beneath our feet, in some odd way it felt like we were all together again. Finally, the heavy flow of tears began to ebb, allowing me to turn around and find the strength to leave. Before I could, Eric gently grabbed my hand, placing a kiss inside of my shivering palm and another on my tear-stained cheek. I leaned in slightly before reluctantly pulling away, knowing that if I stayed, I wouldn't be able to walk away again. I walked away. Never looking back as I headed back to my car to allow him time with our son.

I was flying down highway 288, weaving my way towards 610 when Dominic called me. Though I tried to disguise the hurt in my voice I knew that he had heard it.

"What's wrong beautiful?"

"Nothing."

"Are you sure?"

"What's up?"

"I would like to know if I can see you today."

"Sure, I'm free now."

"Great, meet me at Mama's Oven on S. Main?"

"Sure, I can be there in 10 minutes."

Dominic was already there when I arrived, smiling brightly as he helped me get out of my car. The joke was not lost on me; apparently, he'd learned his lesson from our encounter at Pappadeaux's. I tried to return the smile as I greeted him back, nearly falling into his arms as he gave me a brief, yet firm, hug. We walked inside and were soon seated, and his smile began to slip as continued to study my ashen face.

"What's wrong?"

"Nothing, why do you keep asking me that?"

"Victoria, I saw your beauty through dark tinted windows the night we met, I can hear the pain in your voice that you're doing a great job of trying to disguise and I can see the tears in your eyes, even through the dark shades you're wearing.

If you don't want to tell me, then just say that but don't keep lying unnecessarily."

I was speechless. I had never felt so exposed in my life. But I also wasn't accustomed to anyone being so persistent either, making it oddly refreshing. Finally relenting, I admitted where I'd been.

"I just left the cemetery."

"My apologies and condolences."

"Thank you."

"Do you mind if I ask whom it is that passed away?"

"...my son."

"Damn sweetheart!"

Thankfully, the waitress appeared to take our order, so I didn't have to answer any other questions. After ordering our food, the conversation became lighter as we chatted about everything except what was really on my mind, a welcome distraction. I began to learn more about him as he disclosed that he was an entrepreneur, the owner of a sports bar, a barber/beauty salon, and a construction company. He'd never been married and was the father of three, the youngest of which is the same age as my son. Or rather, the same age my son would've been. According to him he was both single and extremely private; meaning we both had a few things in common. Standing tall at 6'4, his skin was as smooth and rich as milk chocolate.

Articulate and undeniably intelligent, the conversation flowed effortlessly as I tried to stop admiring his warm, intoxicating, smile. After we finished our meal, Dominic escorted me out of the restaurant, making plans to meet for breakfast the next morning as he walked me back to my car. Exchanging goodbyes, he pulled me in for a hug, holding me tight as his cologne and arms wrapped me in a soothing cocoon, I was reluctant to depart from. I'd never been a morning person, but I suddenly found myself looking forward to breakfast. 'It is the most important meal of the day' I thought to myself with a smile. I was so wrapped up in the legal litigation surrounding my son's death, that my 22nd birthday came and went with no fanfare. I hadn't even registered that my birthday had passed until after the proverbial dust had settled.

Now my 23rd birthday had arrived, and for the first time in my life, I hated the day I was born. May 27, 2005 should have been a great day for me. But there was nothing to celebrate. Instead, my life had become a literal timeline of BC and AC - 'Before Colin and After Colin.' Looking at the double stacked Styrofoam cup in my hand my eyes began to fill with tears as I shook my head defiantly, refusing to shed any tears. I was startled by the doorbell, the sound piercing the air as I looked around in confusion. Home alone, I had no clue who it could be. In fact, I'd specifically informed those around, of my current mood, informing them know that I wanted to be left alone. My parents practically begged me to attend our family reunion in La Grange with them. They didn't want to leave me alone. I forced them to believe that I would be extremely busy with work and so I couldn't possibly go with them. Annoyed by whoever had decided to disregard my wishes, I forced myself to get up as the bell continued to ring repeatedly. Whoever it was, they weren't giving up. Forcing myself up from the comfortable spot of misery I'd made on the floor, I made my way to the front door, snatching it open only to be shocked by the figure that stood on the other side. If I would've bet my last dollar that it would be Eric, I would now be completely broke. Giving me an awkward half smile, I closed my mouth as I struggled to compose myself.

"Hey Vee."

"Hi Eric."

"Are you busy?"

"No, I'm not."

"Do you have plans for later?"

"No, Eric, why?"

"Look man, I don't want to fight. Will you put this blindfold on and ride with me? I got you something for your birthday."

"What? Why do I have to put on a blindfold? Since when do you want me to ride with you anywhere?"

Feeling a familiar wave of anger rising inside of me, as I began to protest, Eric cut me off. Determined not to have the day go south and down the drain he asked quietly, "Please Victoria...please."

"Fine," I huffed.

Turning around to grab my purse and keys, I did a quick scan of the living room before walking out the door, locking it before following Eric to his car. Holding open the door for me, once I was firmly seated in the passenger seat, he placed the blindfold over my eyes.

"So, you're sippin' drank solo now?" he asked me as he entered the driver's side. Unable to see I spat out, "Leave me alone Eric. It's not up for discussion."

Riding in semi-silence, with only 50 Cent in the background rapping about getting money the ski mask way, after roughly 20 minutes I felt the car slow and come to a stop. I heard a click as Eric unbuckled his seatbelt and opened the driver's door, tensing as my own door opened and he helped me out of the car. Still unable to see, my ears were on high alert as I heard the pulsing sound of music blasting loudly out of wherever he'd taken me to.

Instantly, I became irritated, thinking that if he'd taken me to a club, I was going to literally attack Eric. I prayed that this wasn't the case. Prayed that even he wasn't that stupid. Finally, he removed the blindfold, revealing our location: Big City tattoo shop. Feeling completely lost, I turned around and asked Eric pointedly,

"What are we doing here?"

"Just wait and see," he replied with a slight smirk. Irking my soul even more. Rolling my eyes, I sat down in silence waiting briefly as a tattoo artist came out and beckoned for us. Taking us in the back to his booth, I belligerently shook my head no when he asked me to sit down. Incredulous, there was no way I was getting another tattoo.

"What the fuck is wrong with you Eric?! I'm not getting matching tattoos with you!"

Genuine shock and horror spread across his face,

"We're not getting matching tattoos!!"

Sensing the situation was about to go left, the artist suddenly pulled out a small sketch, revealing an exact replica of the last photo that Colin had ever taken - a family portrait of the two of us. Stunned and taken aback, I found myself speechless. Eric had given me a gift more precious than even he knew, paying for our son to be permanently imprinted on my skin in the same way that he was already etched on my heart. In all my 23 years, I'd never received a gift as valuable as this. Hours later, Eric was turning back into my driveway. Things were so odd and awkward between us, still, I felt inclined to at least say thank you. Eric and I had once been best friends and he'd been there for most of my firsts in life. We used to talk multiple times a day, even after moving in together. We used to date. Used to joke like buddies and through it all had survived the struggle of becoming young parents while forging our own paths in life. I couldn't help but feel pain at where life had taken us; it shouldn't have been like this. Wasn't supposed to be like this. Turning to look at him directly, perhaps for the last time, I stared into his eyes and whispered, 'thank you.' Nodding his head in response, I took that as my cue to exit. As I opened the door to exit Eric grabbed my arm, pulling me into him and kissing me with a passion that I had never felt before; igniting a yearning deep inside of me that felt like a fire slowly warming me from within. When we finally broke apart, I was breathless.

"I love you, Simone."

Finally pulling myself away from the car, a single tear fell from my eye and down my cheek as I exited the car. Eric only used my middle name in solemn or serious moments, and this was definitely one of those moments. I realized that this was all the closure that the two of us would ever have. His way of saying goodbye...forever.

Eric

Eric arrived back home in a daze. These days, he barely knew whether he was coming or going. He hung out with his friends occasionally and he even started dating. He would spend more time with Monica more than the others, however, he missed his family, missed his son, intensely. And it hurt like hell to accept that neither would ever be whole again. It was gone. Just like that. He desperately needed to talk to someone, but not just anyone. In truth, there was only one person in the whole fucking world that he wanted to talk to, yet he couldn't because life had placed a chasm between them, a rift so big that he no longer knew how to cross it. How to build a bridge back to her. Victoria was the only person he could share these thoughts with, however he finally realized what she'd been trying to get him to understand. If only she would have been patient. Better yet, if only he had listened. A half-smile emerged on his face as he reminded himself that Vee and patience were like oil and water, some things just don't mix. Finally, ready to accept that their chapter was officially closed, he decided that he would have to find another outlet. Another way to release the hurt. Release the pain. Opening his closet door, he moved towards a drawer in the back of the closet; it held just what he was looking for, he picked up his son's obituary, holding it in front of him and staring sadly at the small face that would never call out for him again. Eric's copy was different from the rest, stolen from Victoria after she went to approve the final version. He soothed his guilt by reminding himself it would have been thrown out anyway, thanks to a misprint that made him cherish it even more. Initially, Eric had wondered why there was a blank page in the booklet, an error made by the printer, but now he was grateful for the space. Space he was now going to use to write a letter to his son.

"Daddy's lil man! What's up man? I hope you are okay and I'm sure you are, but I just wanted to take this time to write

you a little something. 'I don't know what I'd do if something ever happened to you' is what I used to always think. But now that you're gone, I have no choice but to know. Therefore, I promise that I will never forget you and I will always cherish the few years that you made my life so bright. I remember always looking forward to the weekend so you could visit your grandparents, but as soon as you left, I would always call just to hear your voice, because I missed you just that fast. This is not the same because I can't call you this time. You're in a better place than me, and mommy, and anybody else here. You don't have to worry about drugs, criminals, diseases, bad credit or any of that stuff. You're where we have to try so hard to get to. God called you home because he knew that you were too special to deal with all of the drama down here on earth. Do me a favor, and let God know that sometimes we mess up, but we (mommy and daddy) meant well and always wanted the best for you. I know that everything happens for a reason, so what I got out of it was this; I wasn't there to see your special arrival, but he called upon me to be there when you left because that's hard and maybe someone needed me to be strong for them. This has to be the most horrific thing I've ever been faced with. But I'm fine now and I just want to be strong for mommy because she is so lost without you. I'll try my best to take care of her for you, but it's going to be hard. But maybe that's why he sent me through the worst thing that could ever happen, to prepare me for the hard challenges in life. I want you to know that we love you, we miss you and one day we hope to see you again."

Love always,

Daddy

Victoria

What had begun as a welcome distraction was now beginning to resemble a relationship as Dominic and I became nearly inseparable. When he wasn't at an occasional business meeting, he always wanted me by his side, and I love the sense of security that he gives me. Dominic is full of surprises. He sent a car service to pick me up and instead of going home; I was dropped off at IAH. Dominic had a ticket waiting on me to meet him in Orlando, simply because he missed me. Once I arrived in Florida and departed the plane, I was in the baggage claim area and I was greeted by a nicely dressed gentleman holding a sign with my name on it. I almost felt like a celebrity. The driver took me to the Portofino Bay Hotel and Resort. My jaw dropped upon arrival. The hotel looks exactly like a village in Italy. After I checked in, I went straight to our room. The room dripped romance. The garden tub held a bay window that opened up into the bedroom suite. I placed my duffle bag onto the sofa that faced the balcony window. I pulled my phone out of my Brahmin bag and sent an alert to Dominic. Whoever invented Nextel phone communication system is a complete genius. The walkie-talkie feature is timeless and so convenient.

"Hey beautiful, where are you?"

"I'm in our room."

"Ok, come down to the lobby and then meet me outside by the waterway."

"I'll be there shortly."

I met him downstairs where he was seated with a group of people.

"You look amazing as always" Dominic said with a smile and then leaned down to kiss my cheek. There was nothing spectacular about my outfit in my opinion.

My knee-high patchwork pointed-toe stiletto boots were

various colors of browns. I paired that with a pair of fitted jeans and a fitted light brown sweater.

"Thank you, baby" I said and smiled.

"Vee, this is Beaux, his wife Kristi and Gabe and his wife Chante... Everyone, this is my lady, Victoria."

I waved as I sat in the seat Dominic, held out for me.

They were waiting for my arrival so that the ladies could be properly introduced and then the guys left us alone to sight see and shop. I did so much shopping that I had to purchase a suitcase to take everything home.

Dominic

They were in the truck for all of two minutes when Gabe started his plethora of jokes.

"Say, Dominic, where'd you get your girl from man? La Petite day care?"

The men doubled over with laughter. Beaux was the first to recover.

"Vee is a cool chick, for her to be so young she has a good head on her shoulders" Dominic stated thoughtfully.

Gabe noticed the look on Dominic's face and interjected.

"She's something special for you to bring her on a trip, you never bring anybody" Gabe stated as he shrugged his shoulders.

"She is fine as hell too" he said with a slight smirk on his face.

"Beaux don't check out my girl man" Dominic stated with complete seriousness in his tone.

"Call them niggas and make sure they're ready for us to pull up, let's get this money" Dominic added. His thoughts still lingering on the young lady that mesmerized him. He still couldn't figure out how a woman as young as she is could keep his attention so effortlessly. She never asked for anything and that alone motivated him to always do any and everything for her. Dominic almost became angry all over again when he thought about how he just happened to call her after she had a blowout on the freeway. He sent her an alert via their Nextel 2-way connection, and she responded so angrily he was caught off guard.

"What?!"

"What?? What's bothering you, Victoria?!"

Her tone changed instantly, "Hey honey... I'm in the middle of something. I'll chirp you in a few minutes."

"Hey, lady. There's obviously a problem so let me help you."

Victoria sighed, "I had a blowout on the freeway and the tow truck driver brought me to a company he recommended and said that he would give me a discount for buying a tire here but now they are both trying to get over..."

Dominic cut her off, "Where are you?"

Vee gave him her location and Dominic was there in 20 minutes. By the time he was done. The tow truck driver left without payment and the tire company had replaced Vee's tire for less than the original price and gave her a full-size spare for her inconvenience.

Victoria

For the first time, in a long time, I felt protected - both physically and emotionally. Dominic was different from any boy I'd ever been with. He was a real man. I even gave up my addiction to drank - finally - because it was a habit that Dominic frowned upon. Luckily, I found that it wasn't hard for me to let it go, thanks in part to my newfound ability to relax with Dominic when I wasn't working. Besides, it became an expensive habit that had started to take a toll on my bank account. But once again thanks to Dominic, that too had improved, as I slowly became accustomed to regular shopping trips, he insisted on spoiling me with. I had outfits for nearly every occasion, which I put to good use during our regular outings. It was nearly 10pm and I was just now slipping on a pair of shoes. I knew that Dominic didn't like for me to drive late at night, so I always left his loft shortly before 11pm. He would have preferred for me to just spend the night, even offering to sleep in another room, yet I declined time and time again. Tonight however, after putting on my shoes, I didn't feel like driving home after all. Dominic had cooked an excellent meal, coaxing me into eating the green peas he'd specifically made for me I had an inkling that his smile had a lot to do with the decision I was finally ready to make. Sliding my shoes back off, I decided to stay. I was exactly where I wanted to be. Walking into the kitchen, I found Dominic washing the dishes as I crept up behind him to explain that I had decided to stay. His infectious smile shined brightly, but there was an intense look in his eyes I hadn't seen before. A yearning that I couldn't quite place. Turning off the faucet, he dried his hands off then leaned into me. It was then that I realized just what that look in his eyes was...hunger. Before I could react, Dominic's mouth was on top of mine, his tongue probing and melting against mine as I fell back against the counter. I could hear my heart pounding in my ears as a surge of desire pooled inside of me. Breaking away, his hands slid down my sides as he deftly lifted me onto the counter, finding space between my legs as I opened them for him to stand comfortably. His mouth found mine again as his hand slid into my hair, grabbing it firmly as he tilted my head up towards his. His lips were demanding, firm, yet gentle. Our tongues intertwined again as my hips arched in anticipation. Slipping my hand behind his neck, I slid it down his strong back before moving toward the front, eagerly grasping the growing bulge in his slacks that begged for release. Picking me up again, Dominic carried me to the bedroom as my legs locked around his waist. Gently setting me down on the bed, I sat in a daze as he entered adjoining bathroom and turned the bathtub faucet on. I was captivated and utterly hypnotized by this man. His sexy ass! I watched from across the room as he added bubble bath in, the suds beginning to form and rise as he turned his attention back to me. Suddenly

I thought about the seven years between us, it seemed like a century, but what if…

"You are so beautiful," he said as he gently cupped my chin with his fingers. "…and you have no idea how much I want you." In that moment age was no longer a factor, it truly was just a number, and I couldn't look away from his eyes. Holding out his hand for mine, as I took one of his hands, he used the other to raise my shirt up and off of me. Kneeling in front of me, he slowly unbuttoned my pants, placing kisses across my breasts and stomach as he moved lower, and lower.

"How did you squeeze all that ass into those jeans girl?"
All I could do was blush. I'd never had a man stare at me with such utter appreciation, I felt both bashful yet wanted as I stood in a purple bra and matching panties. Sliding his hands beneath my derrière, he cupped my cheeks gently, palming them like a basketball as I leaned in to kiss him again. Sliding his hands along my legs and up to my thighs, I felt his fingers slowly slide underneath my lacy panties. His fingers eagerly sliding inside of me as I gasped in delight and anticipation, moaning into his mouth. His fingers moved deftly, searching for the right spot as they expertly navigated

a sensual assault on my yoni. Caught up in the moment, I didn't even notice that my bra had been removed until I felt his tongue eagerly slide across my nipples. Teasingly sucking one nipple before turning his attention to the other. All I could do was bite my bottom lip at the sheer pleasure that I was experiencing. Suddenly he stopped, pushing me onto the bed as I lay there stunned. I watched as Dominic entered the bathroom to turn the faucet off, realizing I'd completely forgotten it was even on. Turning swiftly back to me, I tried to raise up and was gently prodded back onto the bed as he began planting kisses on my neck and trailing down as he suddenly snatched my panties off. Now bare, his mouth replaced the thin piece of lace that had once covered me as his tongue slid inside of me, spelling out hidden messages as I began to writhe in ecstasy, my hips moving higher as he took me to a place I'd never been before. A place I didn't even know existed. Clearly his experience went beyond my 23 years. This was not the rapid-fire action that took place in adult movies that Eric and I had emulated. This is... "Fuck!" I don't know if I screamed it aloud or just in my mind. Gently pulling my legs even further apart, he pushed them towards my head as his tongue went even deeper. Unsure of whether I could handle any more, I tried to place my hands on his head, trying to subliminally coax him into giving me a break to catch my bearings. But he wasn't going for it. At all. Thrusting his tongue in unknown places, in that moment I lost my mind as he stroked my walls with his tongue like a phallus. "Ahhhh," I groaned. Switching with ease between his tongue and his probing fingers, soon I was being rocked by wave after wave of pleasure, and finally the type of climax I'd never experienced before as I collapsed back into the bed, drained and wild with emotion. Looking up into his eyes, they showed no sign of satisfaction, as Dominic picked up my quivering body and carried me into the bathroom. Gently putting me into the tub, I watched as he undressed and joined me.

"You taste so good," he murmured, causing me to giggle like a child. My face completely red as he positioned his body behind mine in his huge garden tub and began to bathe me. A new experience that was both different yet loving. It was my first time being treated like such a precious jewel. After washing my back, I turned around to face him, kissing him deeply as I began to return the favor, lathering and sponging him as he had done to me. His 6'4 frame made my 5'5 one seem like three feet in comparison, making me feel dwarfed. Dominic's face held a look of utter amusement as a half-smile crossed my face. After we rinsed and dried off, I grabbed a bottle of lotion off the counter and grabbed his hand, leading him to the bed. Now it was my turn to force him down onto the bed, where I proceeded to rub lotion across his chest, taking extra care as I crossed his chiseled abs and chest before making my way to his waiting erection. My eyes grew wide at the enormity of it, long, thick and pulsating. I smoothly bypassed his hardness continuing to apply lotion to the rest of his immaculate body. I gently nudged him to turn over so that I could massage his back. I walked over to the stereo and pressed play on the CD player. As I strode back towards the bed, Cameo started singing about the Sparkle in someone's eyes. Licking my lips in preparation, I leaned down and wrapped my lips around him, slowing sliding my mouth down to evaluate just how much I could take before I triggered my gag reflex. "Shit, damn girl!" He cried out, grabbing my hair, and slowly pushing me down further.

Breathing through my nose, I allowed him to fill both my mouth and throat as I consumed his deepest sensitivity. Honestly, it was exhilarating, my body becoming invigorated and saturated as I eagerly wrapped my tongue around him. Unable to take anymore, Dominic threw out another expletive before snatching me by my shoulders, flipping me over and sliding himself inside of me. I cried out in rhapsody as he completely filled my femininity. Giving me a moment to adjust to his girth and fullness, Dominic slowly started stroking. In and out, in and out. "Damn, you're so tight and wet" he called out as he pushed deeper inside of me, causing me to moan loudly. Suddenly, he pulled himself out, flipping me over onto my stomach, spreading my legs, entered me, and stilled so that the only movement was him pulsating inside of me like a heartbeat. Shifting me onto my knees as I bent over and raised my ass into the air. I buried my face into the pillow as he buried himself inside of me, stroking harder and harder as I pushed against him. Grabbing a fistful of my hair he pulled my head up, growling, he kissed me intensely as he continued to slam into me, my ass jiggling in a carnal response. Spanking my cheeks, I arched my back as low as I could go to match his rhythm, stroke for stroke. The sounds of us filling the room in a way that excited me even more. "I want to watch you cum all over this dick" he whispered in my ear, as we maneuvered to place me on top of him. Sitting up, we sat face to face as I rode him as Sisters with Voices singing about weather elements and exploding passions, allowing him to go even deeper as I rolled my hips back and forth. We didn't break eye contact as Dominic began to lift me up and down yelling "Cum. With. Me!" I couldn't hold on any longer, feeling another wave of pleasure wash over me as we climaxed together. Still on top of him, I nestled into his chest as held me close. Our heartbeats syncing as our breathing returned to normal. Foolishly, I tried to get up only to find that my knees wouldn't cooperate, buckling slightly as Dominic grasped my hand and pulled me back onto the bed and into his waiting arms.

I jumped up startled. Grabbing my phone to check the time I realized that it was nearly nine in the morning. I hadn't slept that late in years. In fact, I felt completely rejuvenated. Looking over I noticed that Dominic wasn't in the bed with me, and the loft was eerily quiet. Stretching languidly, I forced myself to leave the warmth of the bed. Walking into the bathroom, I turned on the shower and waited for the water to become slightly scalding hot the way that I preferred before entering and closing the shower door. As the steam rose, I allowed the hot water to saturate my body from head to toe, cleansing me as it cascaded across me. Enjoying the feeling of tranquility, abruptly my brain kicked into overdrive as I pondered the status of my situation with Dominic. Would taking it to this new level change anything between us? Would he want a relationship now? Hell do I want one? Instantly registering that I hadn't thought about any of this prior to the consummation of, whatever this is. I felt my stomach ball up in knots as I dried off. Surveying my reflection in the mirror, it was if my body was ridiculing me. There were no traces of ever carrying a child, making it seem, at least in my eyes, as if Colin never existed. I shook my head stubbornly, refusing to allow myself to slip back into that grievous place. Adorning myself in one of Dominic's shirts, I made my way to the kitchen. I found some basic staples and decided that French toast, cheese grits, eggs and bacon would constitute breakfast this morning.

As I began to fix myself a plate, I heard him come through the door as he called out "She's beautiful AND she cooks?" I just rolled my eyes and smiled. "Are you hungry, Dominic?" I didn't have to look at him to detect the desire in his voice as he answered "Yes. I am." Turning around to face him we locked eyes, and I began to feel a familiar throb at the apex of my thighs. Days turned into weeks, then months. And there were few days that Dominic and I didn't spend together. In time he introduced me to his children, his oldest son Trenton would become the little brother I never had, while the youngest would be a challenge for me emotionally. Bryce is the sweetest little boy, but he was so close in age to Colin that a wave of emotions washed over me the first time that we met. Dominic and his family were a welcome distraction from the void in my own life. I was finally in a good place, with a man who loved and protected me. Emotionally, I was finally healing and looking forward to the future.

CHAPTER FIVE

"Vee!!! Over here!"

I felt like I had just walked into the bar on "Cheers" instead of Barney's Billiards, where I agreed to meet my cousin Jason, his girlfriend Nicole and of course my best friend, Stacie.

"Well look who finally decided to finally leave Never Never Land," Stacie quipped, she was always quick with her jokes. I know I've basically been living in a bubble with Dominic, but since he was out of town, I decided to spend some quality time with those closest to me.

"Ha Ha Ha, shut up Stacie. There's no winning with you. If I'm single too long you complain. When I get a man, you complain, geesh" We burst into laughter. "We're going to work on finding a happy medium girl." As we hugged, Jason took the opportunity to throw in a joke of his own, adding "I thought you'd left the country and moved to Switzerland or some shit" as he shrugged his shoulders in jest. I rolled my eyes before giving him a hug as well.

"Whatever, just know that the next round of drinks is on you."

I was having a blast with my crew. It has been a while since I've been able to have a few drinks and talk shit; still, I couldn't help but have an uneasy feeling. I was about to mention it to Stacie when the waitress approached us with drinks that had been sent by a gentleman seated at the bar. Handing one to me, I asked her who had ordered it. As she pointed the guy out, I politely declined. By this time Jason and Nicole were saying their goodbyes but Stacie and I had decided to stay a bit longer, prompting the stranger to take it as his cue to approach our table.

"Good evening ladies," he said as we both replied with a curt "Hello." Introducing himself as Michael, Stacie finally relented with "It's nice to meet you too." Still, it was a bit too chipper for my taste, as that same uneasiness continued to press against my mind. Looking directly at me he asked, "Can I at least know the reason why my drink was declined?" Michael was handsome, but I wasn't interested. I was in a tricky place emotionally with Dominic and had only recently arrived at a comfortable place with being in a relationship. I realized that relationships are hard work, and I am willing to put in that work for Dominic. I looked up to see Michael looking at me inquisitively, apparently waiting for an answer to a question that I didn't hear since my mind wandered off. "My apologies, what did you say?" Suddenly, Dominic's voice came blasting on my Nextel as "Hey Vee? Where are you?!" rang out over my two-way. I was completely startled as it was something we never did, usually preferring to send an alert first. Picking up the device I pressed the button to respond.

"Hey honey! I'm at Barney's with Stacie. How was your flight?"

"Fuck the flight! Why are you out making me look like a

clown? Who is the dude you're with?"

"I'm not out with a dude!" I yelled in total shock.

Immediately I exited the building to hear him better. Unbeknownst to me, one of Dominic's associates had also been inside of Barney's earlier and had taken it upon himself to relay misinformation. Now Dominic and I are knee deep in our first fight. By the end of the call, I was sitting in the parking lot crying, completely at a loss as to why my relationship was suddenly on a "break."

Feeling lost and completely blindsided, I wondered how Dominic had found it so easy to just take what someone else had told him for face value, without even considering my side. I'd never disrespected him, yet here I was being accused of something that was completely unfounded. I'd done nothing wrong. And just like that, it was back to reality. The bubble I carefully built with Dominic now burst as the months started to go by. Eager for a distraction, I threw myself into work and re-enrolled in college, finally making Dodie proud after I decided to pursue music production as my major. Dodie was over the moon, as she'd always felt like I didn't take music as seriously as the other interests in my life. I was simply happy that Dodie was supportive, considering Gospel and Christian music were no longer the main focus in my life anymore. It was my belief that my mother would only support my music goals as long as the genre is Christian and Gospel. That was the impression she gave me. It was tough, but eventually I stopped thinking about Dominic every day. Initially I thought and agreed that he needed some time to calm down, so I didn't call him for the duration of his trip. When he returned to Houston however, Dominic didn't seem thrilled to see me when I arrived at his mother's house to welcome him home. We had a quick discussion about him needing space and I decided to respect that. It was difficult at first, but finally, I was getting to a good place. My life had structure again, which was good for my emotional well-being. Something I was largely dealing with alone as visits and calls to Dr. Terry had become less frequent. Though Dominic had initially been the reason I gave up syrup, with everything I had going on I just didn't have a desire to do it anymore. I still hadn't returned to church, at least not regularly, but would oblige my mother by making appearances from time to time. I tried praying, but soon accepted that I was still in a bad place in regard to my relationship - or lack thereof - with God.

September 19, 2005 proved to be full of twists and odd turns. Just a month earlier, Hurricane Katrina had decimated the city of New Orleans; now, Houston was forecasted as the center of a similar catastrophic event, as Hurricane Rita barreled towards the city. While Rita did little actual damage outside of wind and heavy rain, millions became stuck on highway I-45 North as they tried to exit the city. Traffic sat at a standstill as Houstonians desperately tried to flee, instead finding themselves out of gas, with many forced to go without food and water. It was also the day that Dominic had decided to make an impromptu call to "check on me and my family." Once he had my attention, he took the opportunity to tell me that he missed me dearly. By this time, I had built up an emotional wall that I was determined to hide behind. After telling him that I genuinely appreciated his concern, I revealed that I still don't want to see him. After I ended the call, a scripture that my mother often recited crossed my mind ""I find then a law, that, when I would do good, evil is present with me." While I couldn't recall where the verbiage was located in the bible, it felt odd that, while fitting for the moment, the thought caught me off guard. As the days went by, Dominic's attention became increasingly pronounced, forcing me to concede just how determined he could be when he was focused. Especially on me. It was one of his characteristics that had made me fall in love with him in the first place. I finally gave in one morning. After one of my classes happened to get canceled, he finally caught up with me as I was walking back to my car to leave campus. Seeing the familiar number pop-up on the phone screen I finally answered, reluctantly accepting an invitation over for breakfast. Once I was back in his presence it was as if we hadn't missed a beat, still, to my astonishment, - after breakfast Dominic invited me to accompany him to Atlanta, where he was going to meet vendors in preparation for his forthcoming clothing store. I thought about it briefly before deciding to go. Thanksgiving break was approaching, and it had been a while since I've been able to take a trip. I decided to accept the invitation before I changed my mind. I didn't want to make the same mistake I made with Eric, telling myself that I needed to at least try to fight for the survival of my relationship. For some, it's easy to walk away from people without any regard to the emotional investment, but for me it wasn't that easy. Not with the experiences that I've been through. In truth, I just wasn't willing to give up that easily. In under a year, Dominic had shown more love and loyalty than people I've known my entire life. Despite our mini hiatus, the rest of our relationship had been flawless, thanks in part to Dominic's ability to shower me with attention while also allowing a healthy amount of independence and time outside of each other. He didn't complain when I wanted a night out with my friends, never objected to me going to a nightclub, listened without judgment when I needed to vent, and held me close when I was feeling down. Besides, who wants a fairytale love story anyway? My own life has been far from perfect, more like a roller coaster than anything else - why should my love life be any different?

CHAPTER

SIX

If I'd been paying attention - instead of acting like a petulant child emotionally - I might have seen this coming. But of course, hindsight is always 20/20. The day before we were scheduled to leave, my car was sideswiped by a hit and run driver as I drove down 610 east. So, I spent the rest of the day dealing with that bullshit, getting my car towed to a repair shop and securing a rental car from the airport. I should have canceled something instead of trying to be superwoman, instead choosing to knock out another recording session before I headed out of town with Dominic.

Thanks to miscommunication I'd arrived at his loft late, finding Dominic slightly irritated that I was so late. He hated driving at night. I was excited. I love road trips. We were going to stop in New Orleans on the way. Naturally, it wouldn't be the same since the city was still recovering from Hurricane Katrina, however the spirit of the city would still be intact. Dominic made a particularly good point; however, this trip would either keep us together or reveal that we needed to go our separate ways. Finally, ready to go, he put his luggage in the trunk of the rental car while I stuffed my purse underneath my legs in the passenger seat, and my duffle bag in the backseat. Soon, it was time to hit the highway. For the first leg of our journey - Houston to Baton Rouge - Dominic drove and I served as the unofficial radio operator. We didn't do much talking as I sat preoccupied with a game on my phone, passing the time and later napping as we inched closer to Georgia.

Once we arrived in Baton Rouge, I was well rested and totally famished. As Dominic pulled into a gas station to fill-up the car, I made a beeline for the adjacent Taco Bell, anxious to secure food for the both of us and get back on the road. As I made my way back to the car, I noticed Dominic talking with two men at the gas pump. Approaching the car, Dominic requested that I drive to a hotel for the night. I reluctantly agreed, since I hated driving in areas, I was unfamiliar with at night. We finished eating and I sat in silence as Dominic threw away all the trash, starting the car again in an effort to find a hotel. As I pulled away from the gas station, Dominic expressed "Baby, I'm real glad you decided to come with me, I've missed us." Smiling, I told him that I was glad that I'd decided to come as well. "Who were those men you were talking to?"

"Just a couple dudes asking for directions."

For some reason, his answer left me feeling disturbed. Merging back onto I-12, I noticed a sign indicating that a few hotels were just a few exits from where we were. Settling back into a steady groove, Dominic was flipping through CDs when a car suddenly pulled up behind me, its distinctive red and blue lights causing my heart to stutter.

Dominic instantly became annoyed, asking "What did you do?" Replying that I hadn't "done" anything, I looked for a space to safely pull the car over, coming to a stop on the shoulder as I brought it to a complete stop. It started to drizzle rain as an officer approached the vehicle, instructing me to exit the car. I was caught off guard by this summons. I've received traffic tickets here and there but have never been asked to step outside of a car before. Yet here I was exiting the car. Reaching in the backseat for my coat, I opened the door and complied with the officer's request.

"Ma'am, do you know why I pulled you over?"

"No, I do not."

"You illegally left your lane a few feet back."

"Illegally left my lane?"

"Yes ma'am, do you mind giving me permission to search your vehicle?"

"Search the vehicle?! Why?"

"Yes or no ma'am or we can wait for the K-9 unit."

I was at a total loss for words, not understanding how the officer hadn't even bothered to ask for my license or registration. Yet here he was, shoving a document in my face and demanding I give him access to search the car. Now it was my turn to be annoyed; I felt as if my rights were being violated and I have never experienced a traffic stop like this before. Trying to remain calm, I asked "How long will it take the K-9 unit to get here?"

"It'll be about 45 - 60 minutes ma'am."

Now indignant, I struggled to remain calm as I repeated "45 minutes to an hour?!?!"

Snatching the clipboard from the officer angrily, I scribbled my name onto the form. I was tired, it was a cold night and the rain had begun to pick up slightly; a recipe for disaster as it pertained to my nerves. Now it was Dominic's turn to feel irritated and he was visibly so as the officer asked him to exit the car as well. Walking over to where I stood shivering in front of the police cruiser, he asked me "What's going on?"

"I have no clue," I told him. "They want to search the car."

Leaning against the car, Dominic pulled me into him, wrapping me in his coat as he held me in his arms. It seemed like the officers were taking forever and I was already formulating a rant in my head that included filing a formal complaint with whatever jurisdiction they were with. I figured a number of violations had been made in this situation. Holding Dominic tightly, my back was turned to the officers when I suddenly felt him pull away from me. The next thing I knew, both officers had pulled their guns out and had aimed directly at us, yelling "Get on the ground!" "Get the fuck on the ground, now!"

If you've never had a gun put in your face before - and I hadn't - then I'll be first to tell you that life will start moving in slow motion. Dominic immediately did as they commanded, but I was stuck. All I could do was focus on the gun that was held stiffly, coldly in front of my face; petrified by the fact that one false move could potentially prevent me from leaving alive. Then, Colin's face flashed before my eyes, confirmation in my mind that I was indeed, about to die. At that precise moment Dominic called out my name, bringing be back to the present as I snapped out of it and slowly began to lower myself to the ground. Laying face-down, I was handcuffed as one of the officers read me my Miranda rights. Ironically, he sounded just like all police do on TV. But this wasn't Law & Order, it was my life, and suddenly it had gone to shit. Also, ironic, was that all of a sudden Dominic had so much to say proclaiming "Baby, don't panic. We'll be straight in a few minutes." I was too shocked to panic, instead curiosity coursed through my veins. Baffled and traumatized, at that point I still didn't truly understand why I'd been pull over, let alone been detained.

I've never been arrested prior to this moment, let alone in the back of a police car, yet here I was. While the officers were occupied with whatever they were doing, Dominic was busy on his Nextel two-way informing whomever was on the other end that we'd been "jammed up" as he put it and that once we arrived - at whatever station they were taking us to - that he would call them back to come pick us up. In my naivety, I believed that this was some sort of horrible mix-up, assuming that at worst I'd be headed back to Houston within the hour. We were taken to St. Tammany Parish substation, but I still had no clue just where in Louisiana we actually were. Once we entered the station we were immediately escorted to different rooms, I couldn't hear anything coming from the room they'd taken Dominic to. Then I heard a door open, and his voice angrily pitched as he exclaimed "The earth is my turf..."

"What the hell does that mean?" I wondered.

Now it was my turn, as a man entered the room, introducing himself as Detective Ardoin. Sitting across from me, he seemed to admire my composed demeanor, but in reality, I was a mess. I had absolutely no criminal background and it was obvious that I'd never even been arrested before and despite my calmness, once the seasoned detective looked in my eyes it was obvious that I was indeed afraid.

"Miss Gafford, may I call you Victoria?"

"That's fine."

"Can I get you some water or soda?"

"No, thank you."

A uniformed officer then appeared in the room. Det Ardoin instructed him to remove the handcuffs from around my wrist before the cop retreated, leaving the two of us alone in the small room. I ascertained that I was in an interrogation room, but still have no clue why.

"Do you know why you're here?"

"No, I do not."

"Well, first let me reiterate your Miranda rights and then we'll get to the situation at hand."

Det. Ardoin read my rights and then asked if I understood.

"Yes, I understand."

"Victoria, I want you to know that as long as you cooperate with me, I'll cooperate with you. So keeps that in mind going forward. You were arrested because the officer that pulled you over found what appears to be six kilos of cocaine, allegedly."

"WHAT?! Six keys?!? Of... cocaine?!!"

I suddenly felt faint as the room started to spin as I struggled to stammer out a response. In that moment I couldn't decide if I wanted to pass out or vomit. Maybe both. This can't be real. Someone had to be pranking me. They had to be. I became incredulous.

"Sir! Clearly, this department is dirty and corrupt, and I refuse to sit idly by while you try to plant your tainted drugs on me. I don't do drugs. I've never sold drugs and I've never even been arrested!" My voice beginning to rise and crack as the gravity of the situation began to sink in. Ashton Kutcher wasn't coming. This wasn't P'Unkd and I wasn't dreaming. I began to plead, "I've never even been asked to step out of the car during traffic stop, let alone brought in for...for whatever this is."

A feeling of nausea continued to wash over, as I struggled to comprehend what was happening to me. Still defiant, I reasoned there had to be some sort of mistake, a prank of some sort. But in my heart, I was starting to realize that it wasn't.

****

Watching her in silence, Det. Ardoin's gut told him that she was telling the truth, but he couldn't reconcile how a young woman as poised as her had ended up in a car with that much cocaine.

Unfortunately, he'd seen this type of situation before. Experienced drug dealers would often find a cover to transport their product; the other party was typically completely innocent and in the dark or compliant and culpable. He now had to ascertain which category Victoria fell under. Staring across the table he could tell that beneath the confusion, and anger, she was genuinely scared. Looking down he scanned the profile sheet he'd been handed again; she was only 23 years old, and his own children were older than she is.

"Victoria, what is your relationship with Mr. Santiago?"

"My relationship? I honestly don't know where we stand right now. We were in a serious relationship some months ago but then we broke-up over a small miscommunication. We were using this trip to figure things out."

"I see. How well do you know him?"

"As good as anyone can know a person, I guess. We haven't known each other for years, a little under a year I'd say. Why do you keep asking me about Dominic?" As his name left her lips, the implication finally registered in Victoria's mind. Det. Ardoin could see the tears welling up in her eyes as he told her "Dominic Santiago has an extensive criminal background..."

She cut him off "He owns a sports bar!"

Knowing that she needed to hear this information. He ignored her and continued. "Mr. Santiago has previously served time for aggravated robbery."

"He's opening a clothing store!"

"He has numerous drug offenses..."

"He's a great father!"

"He also has aggravated kidnapping charges."

"Dominic said that he loved me... I don't even know him."

Realizing that he'd finally broken down her defense, he reasoned that she would now give him the information he needed to close this case. He prodded, "So, who do the drugs belong to Victoria?"

"I don't know who they belong to. I didn't even know that

were there. All I know is that none of it belongs to me."

Victoria

Over the next hour, I answered all of Detective Ardoin's questions, blindly believing that if I did the right thing - as my mother had preached all of my life - that at worst case I'd spend the rest of the night trying to find a ride back to Texas, since the car I rented had been impounded. Tired and frustrated, I was literally dumbfounded. Six kilograms of cocaine?! How could I have spent so much time with Dominic only to learn I really didn't know him at all? Aggravated kidnapping and robbery? What the fuck. He was always so protective of me, but then again it might explain why he'd often time be so intense. Now I was wondering if everything was a complete lie. Finally pushing himself away from the table, Det. Ardoin told me "Ok, hold tight. I'll be back shortly."

But he never returned. Instead, female officers entered the room and instructed me to stand-up and face the barren wall. It didn't take a rocket scientist for me to figure out what was now happening. Unbeknownst to me at the time, Dominic refused to take ownership of the drugs, so even though the officers knew exactly who they belonged to, they had to arrest me as well. An unwilling pawn in a game I didn't even know I was playing. Handcuffed again, I was escorted through the station and outside into a waiting, marked police car. Placing me inside of the vehicle, I was reunited with Dominic, who was also in handcuffs.

If looks could have killed, in that moment I would also be charged with capital murder, as my eyes shot daggers at the man, I now realized I knew nothing about. My "great protector" had officially become my transgressor. I was struggling to understand just what that meant for me. Dominic even had the nerve to ask if I were ok, assuring me that we would both be free by morning. Rolling my eyes, I glared mutely out the window and tuned out the heated discussion between the officer in the passenger seat and Dominic about his repeated use of his cell phone as the other officer transported us to the St. Tammany Parish Jail. A large grey building devoid of any life or signs of happiness, perfectly befitting my mood. I finally felt as if life had broken me. Taking us inside, my coat and purse were confiscated, and I was fingerprinted and placed inside of a holding cell. The heavy cell closed behind me. The deafening 'clink' of the large door rang in my ears as I surveyed the empty holding cell, I realized that I was all alone. The room, if it could be called that, was all concrete except for the combination toilet and water fountain stationed in a corner. Regardless of being thirsty, I gagged at the very thought of drinking from anything that was connected to a toilet. There was no barrier to use the toilet in private either. I finally began to register that I was in jail, and I had no clue how I was going to get out. Then a round face popped up on the other side of the bars, as an officer opened the door to inform me that breakfast would be served in a couple of hours before slamming it shut again. I was now officially all alone. I stood, stuck to the spot they'd left me in, for what seemed like hours, wondering how my life had come to this. I tried to think of any red flags I may have missed but couldn't think of anything. What would my mother say? With a sinking heart I suddenly thought of my mother. MY MOTHER?! Dodie didn't even know that I had left Houston, and of course, in my haste to hit the road with Dominic I forgot to leave a note. Eyeing the pay phone attached to the wall, I lunged towards it and snatched the handle. But as my fingers began tapping the familiar numbers I paused. How was I supposed to call and tell my 71-year-old mother, at the crack of dawn, that I am in jail...in another state, when Dodie probably assumed that I'm just at my boyfriend's house, safe and sound? Dejectedly, I hung up the phone, deciding to give Dominic the opportunity to be a man of his word and get us out of here. Maybe I wouldn't have to tell my mother anything at all, until I returned home. Lying down on the cold slab of concrete that would suffice as a bed, I tried to close my eyes against the bright florescent lights that inundated the room. Cold and alone, for the first time in months... I began to pray.

It was the week before Thanksgiving and I'd officially

been in the custody of St. Tammany Parish Jail for 14 hours, give or take. After initially deciding to put it off, all I could think about now was how I was going to make this call to my mother. In that moment, I realized that there absolutely is a feeling worse than death - it's called disappointment. I knew that my mother would be full of that, and hurt, once I called to explain my current predicament. Taking a deep breath, I began to dial the number again before I lost the little bit of courage that I had. As the phone began to ring, I could hear the pre-recorded message that allowed me to state my name at the beep. Dodie answered on the second ring. After being prompted to press nine to accept the charges, we were finally connected, and I heard my mother's worried tone come across the line.

"Victoria! Are you ok? Where are you? What happened? How long have you been there? What's going on?"

Tears formed in my eyes at the thought of the stress I was placing on my elderly mother. I instantly became enraged at Dominic and at myself. Trying to disguise the hurt, fear and trepidation in my voice I answered "Hey mommy. I'm okay. I'm in Louisiana. There's been some type of mix-up and I just didn't want you to worry Mommy."

"Do you have a bond?"

"Yes, ma'am…"

"How much is it?"

I paused, knowing that what I was about to say would be the final dagger in her heart. "It's a hundred thousand dollars."

"Oh My God, in Heaven!" As I heard her break down and start crying, the tears in my own eyes began flowing like a river bursting through a dam.

"I'm so-so sorry mommy! I didn't mean to disappoint you. You didn't raise me to be here."

"Girl, you are not a disappointment. I just don't want anything to happen to you!"

"I'm a big girl mommy, I'll be fine."

"Baby, momma loves you and I'm going to keep praying for you. This is your prodigal journey and now you're in God's hands. I pray that He continues to protect you in Jesus Christ's name."

"Th-"

Suddenly the call was disconnected. Placing the phone back on the hook, I slid down with my back against the wall, crying like a baby. I'd been there four days when the holding cell opened with a clang, allowing a deputy to step in and scream for me to stand-up and follow her. I instantly became excited, thinking that Dominic had kept his word and we are finally going home. That joy soon turned to horror, as the deputy instructed me to remove all of my clothing from head to toe and handed me a washcloth, soap, and a pair of brown chunky plastic slippers. Pointing towards the corner, the deputy pushed me towards it and said, "Shower is over there, press the silver button to turn it on." I gaped at her blankly, who then informed me that if I refused to shower, I'd be returned back to the holding cell. Trying to shield my body as much as I could, I angled myself sideways as the water shot out, trying to hide my naked body as best I could. I felt utterly exposed. To add insult to injury, after my shower was done, I was given a black and white striped shirt with matching pants to put on. My bra was confiscated as I was informed that I couldn't put it back on because it is red and only white undergarments were allowed. I stood in silence as I was given a pillow, two sheets, a plastic mattress, plastic cup, a plastic spoon/fork combination called a spork and a second pair of striped clothes. They allowed me to keep my S. Carter sneakers because the shoes are mostly white.

Holding my new items, I followed the deputy down a series of hallways until we finally reached a heavy, sliding blue door.

the one in the holding cell. "Open dorm A door." stated the guard boisterously. The door slid open; I was escorted into a cold, dormitory style room, filled with long rows of steel bunk beds. After assigning me a top bunk, the deputy watched and waited for me to settle in and briskly exited the room. As I watched the dorm door close, I climbed up onto my bunk, laying on my back and closing my eyes, I wished that it were a dream, but I finally came to accept that it was not. I, Victoria Simone Gafford was now confined to the custody of the state of Louisiana and there wasn't a damn thing that I could do about it.

"Our Father who art in heaven, hallowed be thy name.
Thy kingdom come. Thy will be done on earth as it is in
heaven.
Give us this day, our daily bread, and forgive us our
trespasses,
as we forgive those who trespass against us, and lead us

*not into temptation, but deliver us from evil. For thine is the
kingdom, and the power, and the glory, for ever and ever…"*

I don't know why I thought that I would feel different or
that maybe some miracle would happen, like the door
magically opening for me to leave. Finally, I drifted off to
sleep and it would be almost a day later before I woke up
again. On the plus side, the dormitory meant I now had
more space to move around in. There was also a TV, which
I quickly learned was controlled in shifts by those that
cleaned the common areas of the dorm. Waking up just
after breakfast, I hopped down from my bunk and
immediately set out to find a phone. I had to call Dodie.
She didn't sound like her usual high-spirited self, not that I
expected her to, especially considering the circumstances.
As we were connected, I asked,

"Hey mommy, how are you?"

"I'm good, just a little concerned that I haven't heard from
you."

I gave her update on my transition inside of the facility and
promised to only call every few days in order to keep the cost

down. Even though she insisted that I call her once a day, we both knew that I wouldn't. I didn't want to be even more of a burden on her than I already was. Then she dropped a bomb on me. Informing me that, "Dominic came by yesterday." I became enraged. My mother had never had the opportunity to meet Dominic prior to this situation, even though I'd met the important people in his life, I hadn't been ready to take that step with him in regard to my own. What the fuck did he want? Not only had he managed to get himself out of jail, but he'd also left me in here, allowing me to spend Thanksgiving in a cold cell without a fucking care in the world.

Trying to compose myself, I asked "What did he want?"

"He told me that he's taken care of getting you a lawyer and also handed me papers that would require me to put my house up in order to post your bond. I'm so sorry Victoria, but I just can't put my home in jeopardy like that."

"It's ok mommy, I wouldn't want you to do that. Don't believe him though mommy, that clown left me in here and no lawyer has contacted me."

"I love you so much, Victoria. Jesus lov-"

And just like that, the call ended. This time however, I was somewhat glad, because I didn't want to hear the end of her statement. Jesus doesn't love me. God doesn't love me. The only people that genuinely loved me were Colin and my mother and even my mother couldn't save me now. Hanging up the phone, I turned around just as another inmate approached me, offering me some of her commissary. I politely declined, not wanting to owe anyone and damn sure not wanting to be anyone's girlfriend just for a damn sandwich. I studied her face, an older woman; she too looked as if she had no business being in here. Introducing herself as Lola she insisted,

"You haven't eaten in two days; learn to accept blessings when God sends them your way. You don't owe me anything. We are blessed to be a blessing to others."

Skeptical, I politely declined again. Lola eyed me sorrowfully but courteously moved to the side so I could pass by. I returned to my bunk and went back to sleep. I awoke to find a sandwich on my pillow. I sat up quickly and looked around the room to see who could have possibly put it there. Not seeing anyone watching me, I finally relented and unwrapped the sandwich, greedily consuming it as if it were my last meal on earth. And for all I knew, it could be. That night I lay in my bunk unable to sleep, listening to the steel bars and doors close as I stared in the ceiling. I contemplated my mother's words as "Jesus loves..." echoed through my mind. Jesus loved who? Not me he didn't! When I got molested, did Jesus love me? When I buried my only son the year before, did Jesus love me then? When I was raped shortly after his funeral, did Jesus love me then? When I sat in a courtroom and watched the judge give the asshole that murdered my son nothing more than a slap on the wrist, did Jesus love me then? Now I was in jail in another state, miles away from every single family member and friend that I had. But Jesus loved me?! Bullshit. I'd tried praying when I first arrived in jail, still, nothing had changed. But as the tears began to flow again, a voice just as clear as a warm, sunny day rang out throughout my head. Asking me,

"Did you really pray with a sincere heart? Did you really try to reach me?"

The answer was no. It was then that I had an epiphany, was this was the pivotal moment that momma had always told me about? The moment when you meet God, on your terms, and form your own relationship with Him. There was no eloquent prayer that came from me like the people at church, there was no thee, thou and thus. It was just me and God. As I'd learned in church, the closet we speak of is not a physical one, it's in the mind. Hopping off my bunk, I grabbed the legal tablet and pen I'd been given and began to pray. Transferring my thoughts, my prayers, to the pad in front of me as everything that I had been taught in church and at home came flooding my memory:

"Come to God as yourself..."

So, I started at the beginning, writing "I'm angry, God. I'm angry and I'm hurt. I feel abandoned. Why did my son have to die? Why am I here? I know I'm not supposed to question you, but why can't I ask questions? How am I supposed to get the answers? Please keep my mother safe. She's all I have left that matters to me. I know that I've broken her heart, please heal her. Help me to understand you as she understands you. Help me to have faith like my mommy does. Keep my father in your grace and my brother too. Help me to understand all of this, In Jesus' name. Amen."

Lola

Over the next few months, Ms. Lola and Victoria would go on to become good friends, the older woman becoming intensely protective of her, taking a liking to the young lady the first time she laid eyes on her - sharing a sandwich in an effort to get the younger woman to eat. Something in her spirit just told her that Vee was different. Lola had always kept to herself, now she watched as the girl tried her best to adjust to life in jail, even giving to others who came in with nothing. But over time, it was a side she felt she had to caution Victoria about, warning her that in jail, kindness wasn't an attribute that needed to be shared so openly. One day in particular, it was a lesson that reared its ugly head. Victoria had been withdrawn, prompting Lola to ask her what was wrong to no avail. Sensing that the young woman needed a bit of space, something that was hard to oblige in a dormitory full of women, she decided to leave her alone for a bit. But as she headed to her own bunk, she noticed a figure hovering near Vee's locker, a new inmate named Patricia. The guards had just completed their afternoon check, so none were in the vicinity, prompting Lola to head over to inquire what the girl was doing near Vee's locker. As she approached, she saw the girl stick her hand inside, swiping a Milky Way before attempting to flee the area. Rushing over, Lola demanded she return what they both knew didn't belong to her.

"Kiss my ass, make me!" Patricia spat back. Opening the bar with a smug smirk, she took a big bite out of her stolen prize. As luck would have it, Vee approached just as Patricia was finishing. She watched in shock as Patricia callously threw the wrapper to the ground near her bunk. Victoria turned to Lola.

"What's the problem Miss Lo?"

Lola hesitated before answering, torn between wanting to avoid any drama and lying to Victoria. However, Vee had quickly realized that something was amiss. "Where'd you get a candy bar from Patty? Did you steal it from Miss Lo?"

"Miss Lo did she steal this from you?"

Before Miss Lo could formulate a response, Patty interjected "Bitch, who the fuck is you?"

To add injury to insult, it was Victoria's last candy bar - and Milky Way just happened to be her favorite candy bar. Her voice boomed loudly demanding to know just who the fuck Patricia thought she was talking to. By this time, a small crowd had gathered, as the other inmates waited to see how Victoria was going to react, unsure if they should get involved or not. Quickly realizing that perhaps she'd gone too far, Patricia tried to reason with her. Jokingly entering her own locker, she grabbed a Milky Way and shoved it towards Vee, "Girl, I'm sorry I was just pranking you. Here's your stuff."

Victoria just stood there, staring at her and the candy bar in anger and disgust.

"Nice try Patricia, but this isn't mine. My initials aren't on it." Kicking the wrapper still near her bunk she huffed, "If you'd taken the time to read the shit you stole, you'd have seen my initials on it."

Sensing what was about to go down, Lola rushed Victoria away from the area. Explaining exactly what she'd seen before Victoria had arrived at the scene. Listening intently, once Ms. Lola was done Victoria's response was nonchalant. "Oh, okay," she said.

Turning on her heels, she made a beeline to the back of the dorm where Patricia's bunk was located. By this time, she'd retreated to her bunk, unwilling to address the situation she knew she'd caused. As Victoria approached, she was deathly calm, stating "Return what you stole...now." As the growing audience followed their voices to the area, Patricia found a new sense of confidence, retorting "I can shit it out later, bit-"

Before she could spit out the word bitch, Victoria had snatched the woman by her long, brittle hair, wrapping it around her knuckles in one hand as she balled her other hand into a fist and began to repeatedly make brutal contact with the girl's face. When the woman tried to scratch at Vee's face, that's when Victoria really got angry and slammed the girl hard onto the cement floor. Vee then pressed her knee onto the woman's chest and continued to rain punches to the girl's eyes. Ms. Lola and another inmate named Princess tried to pull Victoria off of the woman, but they were stopped in their tracks by the thick, overbearing cloud of mace the guards began to spray. The burning was too much for Vee to tolerate. She tried to crawl away, but the guards grabbed her and were dragging her out of the dorm. Victoria and the new inmate Patty were taken to the medical room to be decontaminated and then Victoria was taken back to booking where Assault charges were added to her charge sheet. Patty was taken back to the dorm. Apparently because she was a recovering junkie and because Vee chose to handle the matter herself, Patricia wouldn't be charged. Victoria was getting a crash course in what it's like to be black inside the justice system. Patricia had committed blatant theft and got away with it. However, the powers that be, didn't care about that. All that mattered was the big bad black girl beat up the poor little white girl. This perspective is as old as America itself.

Victoria

I shook my head and laughed out loud. I could hear my mother's voice in my head now..."Only you could get a boyfriend in jail"... It was Thursday, laundry day, and as I dumped my laundry on my bed to fold it, a letter fell out of the bag. I quickly glanced around, seeing no one was looking, I opened the envelope addressed to me. Inside were 3 "coke cards" and a letter. Coke cards are plastic cards that resemble debit cards that held enough funds to purchase 4 bottled sodas from the vending machine located in the dorm common room. Then I read the letter...

"Hey beautiful lady! I hope I'm not disturbing you. I didn't get the chance to tell you my name when we met the other day when you were cleaning up in the hallway. My name is Cornelius Arceneaux, but everybody calls me Bones. I'm from Slidell. I think you're extremely beautiful. I'm not judging you, but did you really get caught with all that cocaine? I would like to communicate with you if that's ok with you. I'm sure I don't have to tell you that if you decide to write back that you can't tell anyone and always put your letter inside of a sock in your laundry bag. I hope to hear back from you. Keep your head up, gorgeous. Storms don't last forever."

I was shocked. I thought about the day we "met"... I was mopping the hallways between the dorms. Officer Lefluer had pulled me out of my dorm to do the task. At first, I was irritated; however, Officer Lefluer presented herself as an ally. Apparently, she felt remorse for me because I am the only non-Louisiana occupant at this facility. Because of that and because I mostly stayed to myself Officer Lefluer became cordial with me. She was the one that gave me the scoop on what was going on with my case. Dominic had bonded out two days after we were arrested. He never attempted to bond me out. Dominic did hire an attorney for me though so at least I didn't have to worry about that expense. As officer Lefluer and I were chatting this guy in a green and white striped jumpsuit walked up. He made a request of the officer and then turned to me "Good morning, chere" in a heavy Cajun accent. I only looked up at him because honestly, I've always been infatuated with men with accents. The man, who I now know is named "Bones", wasn't ugly but he wasn't handsome. He has a rugged appearance. His smile is coy like a child's smile. I responded "Hello" and brought my attention back to the mop in my hand. After I finished, I went back to my dorm and now a few days later I'm reading a letter from a man who's essentially a stranger and in my same predicament as myself.

I asked officer Lefluer about Bones the next day.

"He's rich! He was a big-time drug dealer and he got convicted but when they finally busted him, they beat him up really bad, so he sued the department and won. Then the cop that spent years trying to catch him and who was over his arrest turned out to be a dirty cop so now he's fighting to have his conviction overturned."

"Whaat!" I laughed to offset the awkward feeling I had. "So, is he violent?"

"Not that I know of, he doesn't have anything on his record pertaining to assault."

"Oh ok..."

Laundry day arrived and I found myself hurriedly stuffing the sock that held my letter inside of another sock. My heart was racing, and I couldn't understand why. For some reason I felt like what I was doing was wrong in a major way. Maybe it was because I could actually get in trouble if I got caught. There weren't' any names in the letter so that thought calmed me down slightly. When I received my laundry bag later that day, there was another letter and so began the friendship between us. Every week, there were all kinds of commissary items in my laundry bag as well as clothing items. His letters were always encouraging in many ways. It was nice to talk to someone who understood what I was going through. When he sent me the tobacco, I can't lie, I got scared. Smoking was not allowed in the dorm; however, people still found a way to do it.

The comedic irony wasn't lost on me that I had to come to jail to become a criminal. If anyone wanted to make a purchase, my "customers" relatives would deposit the money into my commissary account first and once I received the receipt then I would give them what they ordered. On one occasion, Patty threatened to tell the night shift guards what was going on if I didn't give her product for free and she was swiftly put in her place by a couple of my regular customers that didn't want to lose my access to the product they desired so much. Even though I was in jail, for lack of a better phrase, Life was good. I received a ton of support from back home in Houston. A lot of people from school and work stopped by my mother's home to check on me since I had basically disappeared abruptly. Some people wrote letters and sent money, books, and other items. I knew most just wanted to be nosy and use the donations as a cover to garner information, however I also hadn't realized that so many people genuinely cared as well. Every now and then, throughout the year since Colin died, I always thought that if I took my life, no one would care and those closest to me would be relieved to not have to deal with me any longer. Being in jail helped me to realize that I actually do mean something to a lot of people.

Chapter Seven

The lights hadn't come on, yet which means that it wasn't even 6 am. Yet, I could hear my name being called over the intercom. I was told to get dressed for a visit. I got irritated because what could my attorney possibly want at this time of morning since it couldn't be anyone else coming to visit… or so I thought. There were two men I had never seen seated at the table in the visiting room when I walked in. As soon as I made eye contact my guard went up, my intuition told me this was not going to be good. "Good morning, Miss Gafford. I'm Agent Jones and this is my partner Agent Clemons. We apologize for the early hour however it was imperative that we speak with you as soon as possible. Please have a seat."

"Agents? With….?"

"We're with the FBI-Houston office."

"FBI?!.... What is this about?"

"Well Miss Gafford, this is about you but more so about your connection and relationship with Dominic Santiago. We've been observing him for a long while now and any information you can give us would be greatly appreciated."

I was not in the mood for this bullshit. I had been here for 7 months and I'd made peace with my situation and these clowns decide to come bothering me and basically wanting me to snitch on someone I obviously did not know.

"Agent Jones, I don't have a connection or relationship with Dominic. I'm also sure you know that since you found me here where he left me. I have not heard from him directly nor indirectly since he left me here, so if you'll excuse me…"

"Please sit back down, Victoria. Why are you protecting him?"

"I'm not protecting him!"

"Ok, calm down. I'm not trying to upset you. Will you at least look at these photos and tell me if you recognize anyone?"

I started looking through the photos and I was watching my life unfold before my eyes. The first few photos were of me coming and going from Dominic's condo but there weren't many of those since it was the week before we broke up. There were a couple pictures after the breakup as well. Most of the pictures were of me at my mother's house and at school and work. From the pictures I assumed that they couldn't pinpoint how I fit into his life since I wasn't around much at that point. Then the pictures changed to Dominic at different locations with different women. One woman I recognized as the mother of his youngest child. Just when you think you've moved on, the mild hurt in my heart let me know that some part of me still had feelings for him even after all of this. The last picture was dated from a week ago.

"Victoria? Do you see anything familiar?"

"I get what you're trying to do. You want to try and intimidate me or anger me into telling you something I don't know. As far I as knew, Dominic was a legitimate business owner. I didn't know he had anything to do with drugs until we got here."

"Help us to help you, Victoria. We can make all this go away. We need to locate him, and you can tell us where he is. There's no way he would just walk away from such a beautiful and innocent woman without one word or some form of communication."

"Well, he can… and he did."

"We came here with the expressed intent to help you if you were willing to help us. It's a shame. Good luck with your case Miss Gafford."

Dominic

"What the fuck do you mean man? How did you get removed from her case?" Dominic was practically yelling. His attorney was on the other line sounding completely incompetent. If he would've been face to face with the older gentleman, he probably would've roughed him up slightly, instead he was exiled in Atlanta and reduced to having these conversations over the phone.

"Miss Gafford had the right to request replacement representation. I told you that trying to delay the proceedings in that way was a risky move to take in another state." the attorney stammered, thankful that his client wasn't in his office at that very moment.

"So, what's the status of the case at this point?"

"You're already aware of your pending arraignment in a couple of months--"

"What about Vee?"

"I'm sure I can find out when her arraignment is, however since she also had the cases separated--"

The attorney heard a loud cracking sound and then the phone call disconnected.

"What the fuck is this bitch doing?!!"

Dominic was beyond livid at this point. He had taken great care to set this plan in motion. Initially he felt bad about using Victoria in this way. Regardless of how their relationship ended, he loved her.

Then he reminded himself of her cheating. It didn't matter that she said she wasn't with another dude or that she didn't have sex with the dude. She had embarrassed him. Victoria obviously had no idea who she was dealing with and she needed to be taught a lesson. Besides, he had product that needed to be sold. The plan had been relatively simple. He needed to deliver six bricks to ATL and as always two cars would make the trip, one car would have the real shipment and the other would have a decoy stash just in case either vehicle got pulled over, then the other vehicle would continue to the destination. He never intended to use Vee in this way. However, the young hoes were getting to hip to the game. All of a sudden, chicks wanted too much in regard to payment up front for the risk they were taking. Dominic knew Vee loved him, so he chose to use that against her just to save a few thousand dollars. Victoria is young, no kids, beautiful, intelligent and doesn't have a criminal record. At worse she would just get a couple years in prison. She would bounce back with no problem. He hadn't anticipated that she would go to these lengths. At best, Dominic knew that he had Victoria mesmerized by him and their relationship. He would have bet good money that she would've just stayed in the jail waiting for him to come get her. Dominic was starting to realize that maybe he should've listened to his attorney instead and maybe his plans would be going better. At this rate, her actions would have his case expedited and he'll be back in prison sooner than he thought.

Victoria

June 27, 2006, seven months later. I accepted that I would be in jail indefinitely and created a routine for myself that consisted of reading my bible at least once a day, writing down my thoughts and prayers and writing to Bones and my mommy. I wasn't able to bond myself out because I had no ties to the local community or the state for that matter, so my money couldn't save me. I also didn't have anyone listed as an emergency contact nor had I granted access to my bank account and that couldn't be changed from jail. Dominic did keep his word, in regard to the attorney he told Dodie about.

However, 3 months into being here and I had never laid eyes on the woman nor had the attorney showed up at any of my court dates, I eventually requested that the judge assign another attorney. At least now when I showed up to court, someone was there that represented me. Dodie as always was full of surprises. She was present at my first court date and even came to visit me at the jail afterwards. We cried, we laughed, and I made my mother promise to never come back. It was tough watching my mother leave. I felt like an utter failure. I spent my life trying to make my mother proud of me and had done a good job up until that very moment. As the youngest of six children, I didn't want to ever be a disappointment to my mother. However, I was also learning that the decisions I made, no matter how isolated I felt, always affected those around me. Just as a drop into a puddle causes waves to form that travel throughout the rest of the body of water. This particular day however, I was feeling particularly peaceful, so much so that I even volunteered to clean the dining area of the dorm just to burn off the overflowing positive energy I was feeling. Shortly after lunch and afternoon count, a deputy called my name over the intercom.

"Victoria Gafford"

"Yes, Deputy Higgins"

"Gather your belongings and roll up your mat."

"Why? I haven't done anything to be moved. What did I do?!"

"You're going home."

"What?! How?"

"The judge gave you a PR bond."

"Clearly there's been a mistake."

"There's no mistake, I've already verified the information. Twice. Roll up."

I was stunned with disbelief. There was absolutely no way I was being released on my own personal recognizance. I didn't have any ties to the state, let alone the parish. My bond up until that point had still been $100K. Nothing about this made any sense. It was a mistake. I knew it. I would be another person whom they told this to, only to get to the front and be returned to the dorm once the mistake was revealed. I asked Miss Lola, the older inmate that had become like a big sister to me, to watch my belongings and if by chance I didn't return to save what could be saved for someone that came in with nothing like I did. I gathered up the state property and made the long walk back to the front of the jail and prepared my heart for disappointment.

It wasn't until I was in my own clothes and on the other side of the door inhaling fresh air again that I realized that I had actually been released. I looked around at the trees and the moon and the stars. I dropped to my knees cried and thanked God. I hear a voice whispering my name. I turned around to see Bones inside the fence, a look of longing on his face.

"I'm so happy for you, bae! How are you getting home?"

"I have no idea. My phone is dead and probably disconnected by now. Nobody even knows I'm out."

"So, I guess this means you're going to forget all about me?"

"I don't know what happens from here, but I'll never forget you"

"Be safe, gorgeous... Goodbye."

"Goodbye, Bones"

God alone was the reason that I was now walking down the side of the road looking for a place to stay the night. I was physically drained by the time I found a comfort suites motel. Another blessing was that my credit card still worked. Once I got settled in the room, I just prayed and cried and screamed joyfully. I tried to sleep but I couldn't. I wanted to call my mother, but I didn't want to give her a heart attack. I went through my letters to look for a phone number to anyone that I could call. I found Latisha's number and called her up.

"Who is this?"

"Hey girl, it's Vee."

"Vee who?"

"Victoria?!"

"Are the calls free there, now?"

"Girl no! I'm out."

"Out where?"

"I'm out of jail!"

"WHAT!!!!!!"

We chatted for a while and then Latisha told me to just get to the airport. She would have a ticket waiting for me. I thanked her and we hung up the phone. I was amazed at watching God work in my life. It's hard to see God's actions while going through the rough patches in life. Up until I had become a mother, God was a just figurehead in my life. I didn't have a relationship with him. My mother had raised me to believe in Jesus Christ. Dodie's favorite verse was "As for me and my house, we will serve the Lord." and as a child you do as your parents direct. Once I became an adult, church was just a place to collect a check to pay bills and provide for my son. I had to reach my lowest point in life to realize that God had been there the whole time. In spite of the hurts, Jesus still protected me. What if I would've stayed home that Sunday that Colin was killed? What if I would've seen him hit by that bullet? What if I would've been there to place myself between my son and the bullet? What if I would have been shot along with or instead of Colin? What if I would've made it to the destination with Dominic? What if all of the blocks of cocaine had been real? There were tons of possibilities in those what ifs. One of which would have been my own death. Even though I had tried more than once to commit suicide, what would that have done to my mother? I learned that in all of this, Dodie had made a serious sacrifice in keeping me and raising me. Thankfully, my mother was still alive to see me free again. Early the next morning, I took a cab to the New Orleans airport. As I boarded the plane, a sudden unexpected nervousness took over my body. It was now real that I am actually going home. This wasn't my first time flying from New Orleans to Houston, so I couldn't understand why I was experiencing anxiety. Turbulence however, almost ruined flying for me. It was so bad; I thought the plane was going to drop from the sky. When I arrived at the airport, Latisha was there waiting on me. We screamed excitedly when we saw each other. The bystanders probably assumed we are long lost sisters with the way we are behaving. We got into Latisha's car and headed home. I have always loved my hometown, however today; Houston seemed more beautiful than ever. The downtown skyline is more amazing, even the traffic on I-45 south, leaving Hobby airport was a sight for sore eyes. I feel like a kid in the candy store once we finally reached the Crosstimbers St exit. I could barely contain myself when we finally turned onto Oxford Street. The car finally came to a stop in my mother's driveway, and I practically fell out of the car from exhilaration.

"Thank you so much for everything, Tish."

"Girl, no thanks needed. I'm glad you're back. Get settled in and I'll swing thru and check on you later."

I walked to the door and unlocked it. No one was home. I glanced at the clock; my mother would be home from work in an hour. I decided to shower and change clothes. Every item I had on from my ordeal was thrown in the trash. I never wanted to see those clothes and definitely would never wear them again. I heard my mother's car pull into the driveway, so I dashed to open the garage door for her. I didn't know what to expect but I do anticipate my mother's surprise. The garage door was completely open, and Dodie was gathering her belongings out of the backseat of her SUV. I just watched her in amazement. In that moment I realized how truly blessed I am. At 71, my mommy didn't look a day over 50 and could've easily pulled off mid 40's if she wasn't so fond of her gray hair. I stood absolutely still as I waited for Dodie to see me. I didn't want to give her a heart attack. Dodie closed the vehicle door, turned around and stopped. She softly called my name, probably because she thought her eyes betrayed her. I began to slowly walk towards her who was shaking her head in disbelief. Once I reached Dodie, we were both in tears and all of my mother's bags were on the ground. I wrapped my arms around her, and we just held each other and cried uncontrollably. We gathered ourselves and I picked up my mother's belongings off the ground and followed her into the house. We talked at length in detail about everything. We prayed together. Dodie could see the change in me. Her heart overflowed with joy. I explained that I was only in the beginning stages of my situation. This was going to be the biggest fight of my life, for my very life. Dodie reminded me that she was here for me and we have the Lord on our side.

****

A couple weeks later, I'm finally starting to relax, and my paranoia is beginning to subside slightly. While I was writing a letter to Bones, my phone rang.

"Hey chick! What are you up to?"

It was my girl, Tish.

"Girl, not a damn thing. What are you up to?"

"What are your plans for this weekend? I'm going to North Carolina, come with me."

"T, I don't have money to fly out of town last minute. I'm still fighting this case. Besides, what the hell is in North Carolina?"

As usual there was a boss level dude involved in her answer.

Tish had met a guy and he wanted to fly her out and his friend asked if she had a friend. Of course, we wouldn't have to pay for anything, and had this been a year ago, I would have gone without hesitation. However, my current situation changed my thinking process tremendously. It wasn't the fact that my flight from New Orleans had scared the shit out of me because the turbulence had been extremely terrible. It was the fact that I'd had enough of the fast life.

"Tish, let me think about it and I'll call you back."

"Ok but call me back… for real."

I didn't even waste my time contemplating. I just told her that Dodie would be a nervous wreck if I left like that again. Besides, I was never going to lie or not tell my mother every move I made from that point on. It took temporarily losing my freedom for me to realize that just because I'm no longer a mother, I'm not alone in this world and my actions still impact other people.

****

To say that my anxiety level is severe would be an understatement. I'm preparing to drive back to St. Tammany parish in the morning and I have no idea if I'm coming back home or not. It was my first court date since being released. I don't know what to expect. I've never been through anything like this before. I actually feel worse than when I gave up drank. I keep breaking out in cold sweats, I'm jittery. I'm staring at the clock trying to figure out how I'm supposed to drive eight hours and I can't even sleep for eight minutes. Lying on my back, I closed my eyes and whispered "God please help me. I can't do this without you. Our Father, which art in heaven. Hallowed be thy name, thy kingdom come, thy will be don---"

I jumped up startled. The sunlight radiated through the curtains. I fell asleep saying my prayers. The irony caused me to smile. I got up, showered, and courageously went to face my "Goliath".

Bones won his case, and his conviction was overturned. I sat patiently in the parking lot of St. Tammany parish jail parking lot waiting for him to walk out of the door. When he finally appeared outside, I got out of the car and ran to him. We embraced and kissed for the first time. The kiss left a lot to be desired. After a brief moment we pulled apart and walked back to the car. Once we were settled, I started the engine and headed towards the highway.

"Marry me, gorgeous"

"What?" I turned to look at him and swerved out of my lane slightly.

"Will. You. Please. Be. My. Wife?"

I am speechless. I don't know how to respond to his question. We kept in touch over the last year. I considered Bones a great friend. I didn't find him attractive. He has a good heart though. Even after I left St. Tammany, he still took care of me, sending me money and gifts even came occasionally.

"Where are we going to live, I'm not moving to Louisiana?! What about your kids? What ab--"

"Just say yes. All that can be worked out later. Say yes..."

"Uh, ok. Yes?"

Cornelius leaned in and kissed me softly on my cheek.

"You won't regret it; I promise to always keep you happy."

****

When I introduced Cornelius "Bones" Arceneaux to my mother, she was very cordial. However, once we were alone, she started laughing and not in a good way.

"Little One, don't you think you're moving too fast?"

"Not really momma, he's a good guy. He's pretty much taken care of me since we've been together."

"I don't think you have to just jump into marriage, baby." Deciding to just drop the subject, I moved to put the groceries away. I was slightly confused, ever since I'd been home; she was the one who reiterated that I should focus on different qualities in my next relationship. That looks shouldn't be at the top of my list, as in the past. Cornelius is compassionate and extremely patient. At 5'11" he's not exactly my "type", his head is clean shaven and smooth, his goatee is always immaculately groomed. He's twelve years my senior, well off financially and he cares very deeply for me. I didn't understand my mommy in that moment. I'm sure that where we met is the root of what's bothering her, however everyone in jail or prison isn't always guilty. After I verified that Cornelius was completely done with any and all illegal activities, we were married in October 2006 in a small parish in Louisiana after my court date. My case wasn't on a priority docket so whenever I went, the case was always reset. Cornelius decided to move to Houston, and we bought a home in Tomball. I settled into the domestic life while I tried to figure out what to do with myself since, now that "the church world" knew that I'd been arrested and the reason for it, I was officially a black sheep. The cruel irony is that I spent 8 months in jail wishing I could play a piano again and now I couldn't play professionally anymore because I had become persona non grata. By the time Thanksgiving rolled around, Cornelius seems happy that I am at home all the time. I, however, am miserable. I want to snatch my hair out multiple times a day. Normally I would take my frustrations out on my piano, however even that became a source of frustration. I needed to figure out what to do with myself, like yesterday. I arrived home from my bi-weekly mani/pedi appointment and Cornelius is in the kitchen making his famous gumbo and the house smells scrumptious.

"I want to open a nail salon..."

"Ok babe, whatever you want--"

"I need to do this on my own."

"Are you sure? That's a big endeavor."

"I know, but I plan to start small and just work my way up."

"Chere, I support whatever you want to do 100%... I have a

surprise for you."

He opened the drawer and pulled out a pamphlet size packet. The surprise turned out to be a trip to the Little Palm Island resort in Florida. I screamed, wrapped my arms around his neck tightly and kissed him deeply. Three days later I am so elated, I can hardly contain myself. I didn't realize that it required so much to get there. After we landed in Miami, we took a car service to the welcome station in Little Torch Key. From there we boarded a motor yacht for another hour. Once we finally arrived, we checked in and the serviceman carted our luggage to what I just assumed would be a regular bungalow, however to my surprise, Cornelius reserved the Island Grand Suite for us. My mouth dropped when we entered the suite. It was beautifully decorated; it's 1200 sq ft of peace and serenity. I left the men at the door to make my way to the bedroom. The only thought on my mind is sleep. I am utterly exhausted. I awoke hours later to the sun about to make its departure for the day. I dragged myself from the bed and prepared for a shower. As I made my way to the patio to observe the sun set on the horizon, the sound of running water caught my attention. Cornelius is in the outdoor shower. I instantly became excited. I removed my clothing along the way to the bathroom. I entered the shower; his back is turned to me. I wrapped my arms around Cornelius and laid my hands on his chest with my face pressed into his back.

"I love you, Victoria."

"Thank you for bringing me here" I said as I placed a kiss where my face had been. My hands slid further down his chiseled abs until I reached his manhood. As I unhurriedly stroked his shaft, a shallow moan escaped his lips. He deftly turned around and pinned me against the wall. Skillfully, he placed his lips over mine and kissed me ferociously. My tongue slid across his lip and then I gently bit his bottom lip. Cornelius grabbed my hair, tilted my head to the side and trailed kisses down my neck. I moaned loudly against his ear. The warmth of the water and his hand kneading my breast making me dizzy. I licked the curve of his ear and he raised me into the air.

"Put your legs on my shoulders"!

I did as I was instructed. Cornelius feasted on my yoni as if she was a breathing apparatus. I massaged my breasts while his tongue massaged my vaginal walls. As my body began to convulse, he gently lowered me into his arms and carried me to the bed. Positioning me on the edge, he resumed his amorous vocal conversation with my yoni. After he felt the shivers vibrate through me, he kissed a trail up to my breasts and teasingly traced circles around each erect nipple. When his phallus entered me, a gasp escaped my lips. Every time is like the first time. His ego is wide and long. His strokes are slow and deliberate as if he's trying to commit every sensation to memory. Open your eyes...I love you...say my name...Cornelius...say my name...Cornelius...who's pussy is this...yours...grip this dick...cum for me...I love you too. I fell asleep in my husband's arms. A short time later, he woke me up to have dinner on the beach right outside of our bungalow. We stayed in our heaven for a week.

Then it was back to reality.

Once we returned home, the days passed rapidly. Cornelius and I were like two ships passing in the night. I still had to report to court in Louisiana for reset hearings and Cornelius had his business affairs as well as his family matters to attend to. He wanted to bring his mother to Texas with us, but his siblings were adamantly against it. I sometimes felt bad because, I talked to my mother daily and spent time with her every other day. His mother is in a senior facility 8 hours away in Slidell. I never complain whenever he leaves to go visit her because I know that feeling all too well. Christmas came and went without much fanfare. We spent that holiday in Slidell with his family and New Year's we spent at home with my family. A week later, I held the grand opening of my nail salon, Kismet Nails. After the final attendee left, Stacie handed me a glass of champagne to have our own toast to my accomplishments.

"I am so proud of you, Vee."

"Thank you, Stacie. I couldn't have achieved tonight without you."

A wave of nausea slammed into me unexpectedly. I dropped the glass I was holding and ran off to the restroom. As I prayed to the porcelain god, Tracie cleaned up the shattered glass off the floor.

"Vee, are you ok?"

"Yes, absolutely! I haven't eaten all day; champagne and an empty stomach clearly don't mix."

We laughed and gathered our belongings. I locked up the salon; we said our goodbyes and headed to our respective homes.

A few days later, I noticed that I still didn't have an appetite and I have been sleeping a lot more frequently. After I closed the salon for the night, I stopped by Walgreens on my way home. I thought I was going to pass out in the store. I couldn't believe I'm in the drug store trying to figure out which type of pregnancy test to purchase. My anxiety is in overdrive and the walls are closing in on me. I could hardly hold the box in my hands due to the uncontrollable shaking. I hadn't thought about having other children after Colin. I didn't want any more to be honest, yet here I am dealing with the real possibility that I may be pregnant. Cornelius and I didn't even discuss it. I don't know how he feels, and he certainly doesn't know how I feel. I couldn't go home and take this test. What if Cornelius doesn't want any more children? What if he does? What do I do if I am? How could I betray Colin like this? What am I going to do? I did the only logical thing I could do in that moment. I went to my mom's house. I used my key to enter my childhood home.

"Mommy are you here?"

There was no response. I went to the bathroom, opened the

box, and proceeded to follow the instructions.

Cornelius

He could hardly believe the positive changes that happened in his life. First, it was his lawyer filing a motion to have his conviction overturned and a judge had approved it. Then he was moved back to the parish jail to await trial which was closer to his children and family. He was bumped up to trustee which gave him a lot more freedom to move around as well as conduct the business he needed to handle. The real shock was the first time he saw Victoria. Her beauty was unparalleled in his eyes. Cornelius didn't care how crazy he looked in pursuing her while they were both locked up. He had to have her.

"Hey, are you even listening?"

He glanced over at the young lady sitting next to him. Tiffany was a jump off that he kept on reserve. She would never be his main woman since she wasn't wife material. He didn't believe Tiffany cared either, as long as he threw a few dollars her way. She was even low budget in that area as well. Cornelius had never given her more than $100 at a time and that was always spaced out.

"What's up boo, I didn't hear you."

She continued with whatever random nonsense she had been rambling about and Cornelius tried to figure out how to shake the immense amount of guilt he was feeling. Victoria is beautiful, smart and everything any intelligent man would love to be with. Here he was not only with her but married to her and actively trying to get her pregnant even though he was sure she didn't want to be ever again. He loved that she always had a smile for him even though he could still see the sadness in her eyes. Cornelius also knew that she doesn't love him as much as he loves her…

Victoria

My mother deserved the world, and I was going to make sure that she received any and everything she requested from me. Growing up she preached that if I came home pregnant at an early age, she would put me out of her house. But she didn't. When I found out I was pregnant with Colin she tried her best to deter me from activities that mentally and emotionally, I wasn't equipped to handle. In truth she was far happier that I was when my pregnancy was confirmed. She also warned that if I ever landed in jail, she wouldn't visit or send me a dime, but years later when I did just that - she was right there when it counted. Only then did I realize that she'd simply been trying to keep me out of trouble. Not only was she front and center for my first court date, she always sent money, especially when I needed it the most. But there was no point in trying to repay her because she wouldn't take it. Instead, I transferred the money directly into her bank account. Because she deserved it. My mother found me in a distraught state when she arrived home. I curled up in a ball on the bathroom floor when the stick showed a double line indicating that I am pregnant.

"Victoria! What's wrong? Are you ok?!"

With tears streaming down my face, "Mommy, I'm pregnant."

"Is that all! I thought you were really hurt! Get off the floor and come in here".

We went into the living room and after she sat down, I sat next to her and laid my head in her lap. My mother is absolutely amazing. She allowed me to cry and then after a moment she raised me up, -looked me in the eyes and said "Ok, that's enough. Pull yourself together, tell me what's bothering you?"

"Mommy, I don't want this baby. I can't do that to Colin!

What if Cornelius doesn't want kids? --"

"Breathe, Victoria... Colin is in a better place and he would be happy to have a sibling if he were still here, you already know that. Cornelius is happy with whatever makes you happy and you know that as well. I understand I didn't like him at first, but he's good for you and I see that now. As long as you're happy then momma's happy! Whatever you decide to do I'm right here with you as always."

"Thank you, momma, I love you so much!"

August 12, 2007 Cornelius and I are at a friend's BBQ and it's actually a pleasant evening. He was so excited once I told him that we were having a baby. So happy in fact, he upgraded my ring. 4 carat emerald cut diamond center stone and 1.5 carat trillion cut diamonds on the side in a vintage platinum setting. Cornelius keeps a watchful eye on me every time I move at this party. He's slightly irritated because I'm wearing high wedge heels. I'm more than sure he's going to blow a gasket once he figures out, I'm headed to the dance floor to do the Cupid Shuffle.

All of 8 minutes later, I realize that I am in labor. Cornelius grumbled and griped the entire way to The Woman's

Hospital.

"I don't know why you're so stubborn, why wouldn't you just sit down and relax like normal pregnant women?!"

I just rolled my eyes, "You do realize this isn't my first baby, nor is it your first either" and I flinched from the abrupt tightness of my abdomen. The contractions were getting stronger and closer together.

"That's not the point Victoria. Childbirth is not a game and shouldn't be taken lightly. Women die giving birth and most are black women..."

"I apologize, love" Realizing that Cornelius is making a very valid point, I conceded. I also needed him to focus more on driving and less on me. Upon finally arriving at the hospital, we find my mother and my best friend already there waiting on us. By the time we were placed in a private room, my contractions are 5 minutes apart and I am 9cm dilated. The staff finished their prep work just in time for me to start pushing. I looked around the room at the people who were by my side at the lowest of times and now here during this joyous occasion. I began to cry as a wave of guilt slammed into and consumed me. Colin's face appeared and as he flashed his sweet smile, I heard his voice echo "I love you mommy". Then there was extreme brightness.

Cade Vysean Arceneaux was born August 12, 2007 at 10:45pm. He has big brown eyes like his father and dimples like his mother. I'm watching my mother in awe as she's cuddling him in her arms. Cornelius is in the reclining chair sleeping and Stacie would be back tomorrow to visit her godchild.

"Hey, little one, you're awake?" my mother asked me.

"Hey momma" My smile turned to sheer horror as she arose and started towards me with the baby in her arms. I am not ready. A part of me doesn't want to get attached to Cade. I feel like I'm cheating on Colin. Then I hear his words echo again in my mind.

"I love you, mommy."

My mommy places Cade in my arms and a wave of peace washes over me. All of my fears and anxiety went away, and I knew that we would all be okay.

Chapter Eight

"Mommy, stop"

I paused as my almost two-year-old son Cade, waddled over to me.

"Kiss"

Cade warmed my soul with his demand. I had to squat down to his level to give him his kiss. He smiled and ran back to his father's waiting arms. I stood up and smooth my black skirt down and turned to face my attorney.

"So, once the judge enters the courtroom then session will

begin. As you know, your family members that are witnesses will not be allowed in the courtroom until after they have given their testimony and the prosecutor has had the opportunity to cross-examine."

I nodded my head in acknowledgment as the infant boy in my arms started to stir. Christian Vernon Arceneaux was born two months ago on June 15, 2009. During my Pre-trial period these past 3 years, I'd gotten married and given birth twice. My mother thought I was insane, occasionally so did I. Outside of this whole trial fiasco, life is amazing. I have a loving supportive husband. My mother and I couldn't be closer, and I have a phenomenal career that allows me the freedom to be with my children as much as I see fit.

"Is it ok if my children are in the courtroom?"

"Of course, Victoria. As long as they aren't disruptive to the proceedings."

One of the court officers approached us and said, "DA Collins is requesting to see you and your client before court."

We were both shocked.

"Ok, we will be in shortly" responded my attorney.

Allen Greer was not a big shot attorney. When we first met,

he was reluctant to take my case for many reasons. The main reason in my opinion, is that he didn't believe in my innocence. Even though he's tried to convince me otherwise on many occasions. I cooed with my son as we approached the table where the prosecutor was seated. The prosecutor jumped right into his offer.

"I wanted to give you a final opportunity to accept the offer that was presented. 30 years, parole in 15 with good behavior and I'm willing to remove the "to life" addition if you'll save us all the trouble of proceeding with this trial."

Mr. Greer looked at me and I only arched my eyebrow and continued to soothe my child in my arms.

"My client will not accept your offer."

I turned to walk away when the prosecutor stated, "Think of your baby."

I locked eyes with him and stated, "That's all I'm thinking of."

I exited the courtroom and walked over to my family. I begrudgingly handed Christian over to Stacie and kissed him softly on his head. Everyone looked so somber. I plastered a huge smile on my face and said, "Let's do this!" We grabbed each other's hands, bowed our heads and my mother began to pray.

For the first time in my life, I was second guessing if I should have worn my favorite color. My pencil skirt suit was tailored to perfection. Most people only reluctantly wear black for funerals, however black is my favorite color. The color compliments my complexion and I'm at my peak level of confidence whenever I wear this color. However, as I walked into the courtroom, I began to wonder if I'd subconsciously dressed as the grim reaper to prepare for impending doom. Everything is now in God's hands I thought as the court officer cleared his throat when the judge entered.

"All Rise! Court is now in session..."

Eric

"Baby yes! Of course, I'll marry you!"

What the hell did I do?

He was in shock, somewhat anyway. Although happy that Monica accepted his proposal, his thoughts however, instantly went to Victoria and how everything is going with her case. Tamika kept him updated on Vee's activities. He had to admit, he was devastated when he found out that she had not only been arrested but that she'd been left in a foreign parish in Louisiana. He happened to show up unannounced at her parent's house while her mother was sitting outside on the porch. As he parked the car in the driveway, he noticed Vee's mother was crying.

"What's wrong Ms. Dodie?"

"I'm just missing my baby, what brings you by?"

"I just stopped by to see Vee, is..."

A shocked expression covered her face and some unknown reason caused her to start crying uncontrollably. Eric was completely lost. He put his arm around the older woman's shoulder.

"Eric... Victoria isn't here... She's been in Louisiana...for months...in jail."

"Jail?!" Eric felt his heart stop. He just stared at the woman who was supposed to be his mother-in-law.

"How...why???"

"Some guy that she was involved with had a bunch of drugs in the car and to make matters worse, he's left her there."

Eric instantly became enraged. Who in the fuck is this bum ass nigga that left *his* woman... he froze. Eric was so accustomed to Victoria being his that he instantly forgot that they have been broken up for over a year now. He reached into his pocket and pulled out a wad of cash and peeled off a few twenty-dollar bills and reached out his hand to Vee's mom.

"Here, take this Ms. Dodie..."

"No, Eric that's not necessary".

"Take it, please. Send it to Victoria or keep it for yourself.
I'll be back by tomorrow for her information."
With that, he left, still furious and headed directly to the
very person he knew would have answers, his sister...
"TAMIKA!!!!"
He yelled her name as he was walking up to the front door.

****

He pounded on the front door, too angry to remember to use
his key. "What the fuck is wrong with your stupid ass?!"
she said as she snatched open the door.

"You are what's wrong with me!! Why didn't your simple
ass tell me about Victoria?... So, who is the nigga that got
her locked up?!"
"First of all, why are you even questioning me about
Victoria and her personal life, when you should be
explaining why I have to find out about my baby brother's
engagement from his fiancée?"

His shock temporarily reigned in his anger. He had just
proposed to Monica that morning. He hadn't had time to
tell anyone else, since becoming absorbed in making sure

that Victoria found out from him about this relationship with Monica and not from anyone else. He wasn't expecting to be blindsided by the revelation that she was in jail in the middle of nowhere.

Eric shook his head at the memory and went to the garage and stared at the box that held the letters from Victoria's jail stint. Had Monica not been at home, he would've pulled out a few and re-read them. However, he had to be satisfied with looking for now. Eric wanted to call her or text her, but he knew that she was currently in court. Not being able to be there for her was killing him slowly. He tapped the box twice and then headed inside to get ready for work. Eric silently sent up a prayer that God would allow her to come home. After they both have worked so hard to gain the friendship they now have, Eric would die if he could never see or touch Victoria again.

"Baby, I packed your lunch. Have a great day at work..." Eric pasted a half smile on his face as Monica continued talking. He didn't hear a word she said. Monica is a good woman and although caring for her deeply, he also knew he would never love another the way he loves Vee.

Dominic

The sirens blared, the red and blue lights flashed, and the rear-view mirror was consumed with the bright headlights of the police cruiser. He had just turned onto the feeder road of Eastex Freeway from Florida street, leaving one of his trap houses in 5th ward. Dominic released a semi disgusted sigh as he pulled the car over and waited for the police officer to approach the truck window.

"License and Insurance"

"Good evening officer, sure just a second"

He reached in the glove compartment for his insurance card and then into the arm rest for his driver's license. After handing the items to the officer, he relaxed into the seat.

"I'll be back in a few minutes."

The officer returned to his vehicle and entered the info into his computer. While he was inputting information a backup call came through the radio. He hurriedly scribbled in the data onto the ticket and got out of his vehicle.

"I'm citing you for improper lane usage, your court date is located on the bottom and payment info is on the back" he stated as he handed the ticket, license, and insurance card back to Dominic.

"Have a good evening".

"Ok, officer. You do the same."

Dominic shook his head and smirked, unbeknownst to the officer, there is a fugitive warrant out for his arrest. Being pulled over caused him to think about how he received the warrant in the first place. After pleading "not guilty" at his arraignment in St. Tammany parish, Dominic returned to Houston and never went back. He wondered how Victoria was doing. After everything that went down with them, he still couldn't shake his love for her. During a conversation with his attorney Dominic found out that her trial began today, but that's all he could find out. He wouldn't know the verdict for at least a week. While he never meant to hurt her, there was no way he would've gotten this far in life by falling on his own proverbial sword. Self-preservation came at all costs. He'd done his time and wasn't going back to prison under any circumstances.

Victoria

"You may be seated."

The judge stated in a monotone voice. As I sat down, I briefly looked behind me to see Stacie soothingly rubbing little Christian's back. He's only two months old so I'm sure he's sleeping. My palms were starting to moisten. I glanced over at the twelve ladies and gentlemen sitting in the elevated sectioned off area of the courtroom. Each individual person's face is solemn and unreadable. My attorney gently patted my hand and the prosecutor stood up. "Ladies and Gentlemen, I stand before you this morning with the objective to prove that the defendant, Victoria

Simone Gafford, did knowingly possess 6 kilograms of cocaine with the expressed intention to distribute that product illegally."

While he continued with his opening remarks and during the opening remarks by my attorney, I took very detailed notes. During each witness testimony, I took the initiative to compare what is being said on the stand to what is in the discovery report. Mr. Greer is an awesome attorney; however, nobody is going to fight for my life better than me.

"We're going to break for lunch and then we'll resume after with testimony from the defendant" the judge stated and then banged his gavel.

"All rise"

****

Lunch was extremely awkward. The only people making any noise are the children and myself. Cade wanted to hold Christian and since we're in public I told him no and he doesn't want to accept that answer. "Well, honey at least you won't have to go far to visit me."

I tried to break the tension with a joke, however I only

succeeded in making everything worse. Cornelius just blankly stared at me and my mother started to cry. I stood up and put my arm around her shoulders.

"I apologize mommy, I'm just trying to lighten the mood."

"It's not funny, Victoria. You have a husband, these two little babies... And what about me?"

My vision became blurry as the tears filled my eyes. At the time of my arrest, I was a single woman and childless. Yet that situation is now impacting people that weren't even in my life at the time. Life is so strange. Cornelius broke the silence by announcing that we should get back to the courthouse. We definitely do not want to be late for that.

****

"Do you swear to tell only the truth, so help you God?" the court officer asked.

"Yes, sir"

Up until that very moment, my stomach had been in knots and my palms were very damp, despite the poker face I maintained. I am always the brave one. My mother constantly reminded me of how strong I am. I believe now that it was reverse psychology. I'm grateful for it, because as soon as I sat down in the witness seat my spine stiffened and I transitioned into full protect mode. As I waited patiently for the DA to stop his weak attempt at mental warfare by allowing the tension to build in the room, I focused my thoughts on all that I had to lose. I decided in that very moment that I. Will. Not. Lose...Ever.

"State your name for the court record, please".

"Victoria Simone Gafford-Arceneaux"

"Where do you reside... Ms. Arceneaux?"

"Tomball, Texas a suburb just outside of Houston"

"Is the name you gave for the record your legal name?" Apparently, the prosecutor is attempting to start off by implying I'm a liar.

"Yes, it is. Arceneaux is my married name."

"Oh, congratulations. Are you employed? If so, where do you work?"

"Yes I am. I am the owner and one of the operators of Kismet Nail Salon."

"Were you working there on November 15, 2005?"

"No, I was not."

"Where were you working at that time?"

"I was a freelance musician and full-time student at the University of Houston."

"Were you acquainted with any of the arresting officers or detectives prior to the date of arrest?"

"No"

The prosecutor went on and on with his questions and I remained unwavering. Unlike the arresting officers whose statements were flawed and filled with lies that my attorney successfully pointed out during his cross examination. I maintained eye contact with the jury and spoke clearly and confidently. Once the prosecutor finally ceased his inept attempt to break me down or dismantle my testimony, it was now my attorney's opportunity to redirect the jury's attention to the details that mattered. The prosecutor wanted the jury to focus on who I am now; I and my attorney needed the jury to focus on who I was at that time.

"Mrs. Arceneaux, what was your age at the time of this occurrence?

"23"

"Do you know the age of your former boyfriend at that time?"

"30"

"So, a seven-year age difference?"

"Yes"

"Do you currently have any children?"

"Yes"

"How many children have you had?"

"3"

"What are the ages of your children?"

"deceased, 1 year and 2 months"

"What do you mean deceased?"

"My first child died January 25, 2004"

"Please recall your version of what took place on November 15, 2005?"

I turned towards the jury and began to retell the narrative of that night. I maintained eye contact the entire time. I did shed a couple tears when asked about my emotional and mental state at that time. After I was done, others were brought in to testify on my behalf in regard to my character. Then came the defining moment. The judge declared that it was time for the jury to deliberate. My family, my attorney and I gathered in the hallway to wait. My attorney stated that he didn't think the wait would be long. He was clairvoyant in a way since we have only been in the hallway for about five minutes when my attorney and I were summoned to a conference room. The prosecutor shocked us both upon entering the room.

"30 days parish jail and 2 years' probation. That's my final offer."

Mr. Greer looked at me questioningly.

"I'm not going back to jail under any circumstances."

"This is an exceptionally good deal that I'm offering you, young lady. Don't allow your pride to take you from your children for the next 30 years or life."

"If you felt that strongly about it, you wouldn't be offering anything at all. You want a conviction and I want to go home. I'll accept the probation, transferable to my home in Houston and mandatory expungement upon completion. That's my final offer. Take it or leave it. But I'm absolutely not going back to jail, at all."

The prosecutor gave an exasperated sigh before saying.

"I'll inform the judge."

My knees buckled slightly. I hadn't realized that I had been under so much stress until the threat to my freedom had been removed. Mr. Greer shook my hand firmly and with a smile stated that I shouldn't give up on my dream of being an attorney since clearly my negotiating skills are up to par. We exited the room and I decided to keep the information to myself until the judge made it official in the courtroom. After it was all said and done. I pled guilty to a lesser charge of possession of a controlled substance. The intent to deliver was removed and so was the weight factor since four of the six kilograms of cocaine turned out to be fake. I was given credit for time served in the parish jail and after they finished with the calculations, I estimated that I would only be on probation for a year. My mother almost passed out when the judge was announcing the complete sentence. She heard the words "5 years in state jail" and let out an audible gasp. As we left the courtroom, everyone expressed their displeasure with the ruling, and I happily reminded them that they could've been leaving without me.

Chapter Nine

Am I having a heart attack? is the question that I'm currently asking myself. My heart is pounding so hard that I am beginning to get dizzy. I briefly lean against the wall of the building and begin my breathing exercises. I wasn't this nervous when I gave birth for the first time. I couldn't understand why my anxiety was so high. As my pulse slowed down and my heart united with the pace, I realized that while our communication has greatly improved, I haven't physically seen Eric in four years. We wrote each other a lot while I was in jail and even when I was released, out of respect for my husband I never met with Eric in person. We talked on the phone but not much and only when neither one of us was at our respective homes. When he called me this morning and requested that I meet with him, he had a sense of urgency in his voice. I obliged him and now I was starting to regret it. What if he wants to get back together? What if... I think I'm more afraid of my response to the first question than the actual question itself. While Eric has been kind, supportive and of course clear on his stance of still loving me, he's hasn't actually professed wanting to rekindle our relationship. I gathered my composure and smoothed down my skirt, straightened my back and walked into the restaurant where Eric had been waiting for me.

Eric

He didn't think it was possible, yet in she walked looking more beautiful than ever. Pregnancy had been a blessing to her in more ways than just her children. His mind flashed back to when they initially met at Barbara Jordan High School. Victoria had a beautiful face back then, but she was as skinny as a bean pole. Now?... now she is a gorgeous woman. Victoria's hair is short like Toni Braxton and her body now had curves that were enticing to any man but even more so to him since Eric knew the transition firsthand. He could feel his manhood almost reach full attention and had to remind himself that they were both in a public place and also remember the reason he invited her to the Aquarium Downtown. Eric's partial erection subsided once he thought about the words, he needed to use to tell her the admittedly disturbing news. Inwardly shaking his head, Vee had always had an enticing stride when she wore those high heels but now combined with her curves, she walked with a superior confidence that just left any man in her presence breathless. There were a few distracted male faces at the tables she passed by. Victoria knew what she was doing. Eric stood up to greet her and pulled out her chair. They made small talk and held long glances in each other's eyes. Once the waiter brought the check, Victoria was the one who broke the trance of the evening.

"Eric, why are we here?"

She would probably never forgive him for what he was about to say in the restaurant that they were supposed to bring their son to, had he not passed away on the day they were scheduled to come.

"Simone, I have something to tell you..."

"Look, I think I know what you're going to say..."

"Can you please, for once, let me finish." he paused, and she nodded. Eric gently reached for her hand and placed hers on top of his.

"We've been separated for some years and I know I avoid certain questions you ask, and I also redirect certain conversations.... There's no easy way to say this. I'm getting married and I didn't want you to find out from anyone except me."

Their eyes held each other's stare, but he could see the shift in her gaze and the moisture building. Victoria never said a word. She swiftly removed her hand from his, picked up her purse, stood up from the table and walked out of the restaurant.

Victoria

The tears were streaming down my face before I could exit the building. I was frantically searching through my Brahmin bag for the car remote, the steady stream of fluid trailing down my face wasn't helping. As if that wasn't enough, my nose joined the moment. It didn't help that once I was inside my vehicle and started the ignition, Boyz II Men were singing about the end of the road. I quickly turned the station and then the H-town chick Letoya Luckett began reminding me that I'm not doing this anymore.

"Simone..."

I heard my name being called. Thankfully, Eric didn't see me in my truck. I threw the vehicle in reverse and sped out of the parking lot. The tears flowed my entire ride home. I couldn't understand it. Why does the heart have so much control? As I neared the gate to my subdivision, I looked in the mirror, dried my tears, reminded myself that I have an amazing husband at home. A partial smile eased onto my face listening to T.I. sounding like my husband, saying I can have whatever I like. I shook my head at myself thinking I could've so easily ruined the best thing to happen to me besides my children. Cornelius loved me through my second worst moment in life. He deserves better than the half love I've been giving him. I decided instantly that I'm going to plan a special night for him. Hopefully, I haven't jeopardized everything I've been blessed with.

Cornelius

"Bones, why won't you just leave her and be with me?"

He made a mental note to block her number once he was inside of his truck.

"Don't start that shit again, you knew damn well from the beginning that I'm not leaving my wife. Look, it's obvious you can't deal with this situation, so we're done."

He slid his foot into his shoe. Cornelius raised his glance towards the woman he just finished having sex with. She wasn't as beautiful as his wife. She definitely wasn't as smart. He met Tiffany years before he met his wife. Tiffany was a chick that he became involved with at a time in his life when he was heavy in dealing drugs and not looking to settle down with anyone. As he adjusted the belt around his waist, the young lady got out of the bed and came around to face him.

"No, we're not done! If you even think you're going to break up with me, I may just decide to send a message to your precious wife on Facebook and tell her all about your so-called business trips to Louisiana. I think she definitely needs..."

Before Tiffany could finish her last statement, Cornelius had wrapped his hand around her throat and pinned her to the wall. In a low, steely cold voice he told her.

"That would not be a smart or safe decision for you to make. Like I said, we're done." he stated as he slowly lowered her to the floor. He coolly picked up his keys and left. As he navigated the Escalade truck back towards his brother's house where everyone was gathering for dinner with their mother, the sound of the ringing phone came through the car speakers. Cornelius hadn't realized that he was in a foul mood until he felt his countenance shift when he saw my wife's photo on the phone screen.

"Hey Big Daddy!"

He despised women that weren't prostitutes that referred to their "man" as "daddy". Victoria knew this; however, it was now a joke between them. An ice breaker of sorts. The tone she used intentionally when she said it, is what would cause them both to laugh. She almost sounded exactly like Jasmine Guy's character Whitley on the old show "A Different World". Their affinity for that show is just one of the bonds they share. Cornelius was stuck in her web and they both knew it.

He chuckled, "Hello my love."

Victoria has an infectious personality, especially when she was in a good mood. However, no matter what she is feeling, it transfers to whomever is around her. He didn't think she even realized how she affects others, which is how he knew she didn't feel as strongly for him as he did towards her.

"What are you doing?"

"I made a quick run to the store and I'm headed back to Kevin's house now. I miss your sexy ass, what are you doing?"

"I just put Christian down for his nap and about to watch a movie with Cade. You'll be home tomorrow, right?"

"Yes, my dear, I'll be home tomorrow around 7p."

"Ok, we'll be at Dodie's house, but we'll see you when we get home."

She disconnected the call. Cornelius is not the type of man to complain. He knows Victoria loves, respects, and even appreciates him. For those reasons, he continues to give her the world. Something was off and always had been though. He didn't have all of her, like she's holding something back. His ego just wouldn't accept her not being *in* love with him. About 3 months ago, Cornelius decided to have a fling with his ex. It was supposed to be a one-time thing. After the conclusion of his wife's trial, he thought that his marriage dynamic would improve. The pressure of being a mother again and going through the mental toll of the trial seemed to be what was the hindrance between them. However, a couple weeks before the trial took place, he happened to be at her parent's home assisting Vee's father with some yard work. He'd taken her SUV by default since his wife had absconded with his truck that she's infatuated with. He and his father-in-law walked to the front yard where Cornelius was parked and when he got into the driver's seat there was a red envelope under the windshield wiper. The envelope had Victoria's name on the front written in an unfeminine fashion.

"What's that son?"

"I don't know Pops; it's addressed to Vee." An uneasy feeling crept over him as he flipped over the envelope to open it. Pops waited with curiosity and as Cornelius removed the card inside his heart began to sink.

"I miss you more than words can express. Hope all is well...
Love always, E".

A varied range of emotions went through his mind. From anger to rage to hurt.

"What does it say son?"

"It's a card from that nigga Eric!" Cornelius stated disdainfully.

"Eric, huh?... Son, before you allow your anger to cloud your head. Take into consideration that the card was left on the windshield so that can't mean much of anything if he didn't take the time to make sure it reached her hands personally."

He thought about what Pops was saying but a part of him began to think that maybe the real reason Victoria couldn't or wouldn't commit fully to their marriage is because she's still in love with this clown. He told Pops goodbye and decided to head home. At the end of the day, Victoria Simone Gafford-*Arceneaux* is *his* wife. Eric's clown ass can't compare to him nor the life he gives her and their kids. Once he entered the entrance ramp on the freeway, he lowered the window and sent the card flying in the wind.

Victoria

"Just press 6926907 on the keypad to close the garage door. I really appreciate you for helping me put this in place at the last minute."

After Eric's assistance with bringing me to my senses, I called my best friend Stacie to meet me at Zadok Jewelers in the Galleria to help me upgrade my husband's ring. During the drive there, I contacted Culinary Creations by Todd to put together a private dinner at home for my husband and me. I had to pull out all the stops to make sure that Cornelius experienced the feelings that he gives me regularly. I must prove to him that I am fully invested in our marriage. My parents gladly obliged me by keeping the boys tonight. I looked at the clock and saw that he would be home in 15 minutes. I dashed to the bedroom to prepare for his arrival.

Cornelius

"Soon as I get home, I'll make it up to you…"
Cornelius could hear Faith Evans singing loudly in the garage as he pulled in next to his wife's Rover. He could've sworn she told him that they would be at her parent's house until later. He opened the door, and his nose is embraced by the tantalizing smell of dinner, but as he entered the kitchen, he only saw an unknown man in a chef's coat standing in front of the stove.

"Good evening, Mr. Arceneaux" Chef Todd said with a monotone voice.

Before Cornelius could even respond, he was greeted again…

"Good evening my love"

Victoria was walking towards him wearing the absolute skimpiest undergarments he'd ever seen. The black lace is mesmerizing against her smooth unblemished skin. The bra has her breasts sitting up high like two mountain peaks. The panties have a butterfly shape on the front. She kissed him firmly but teasingly and grabbed his hand and turned to lead him to the dining table...

"Baby, what type of panties are those??!"

Both of her ass cheeks are fully displayed, she laughed slightly... his dick got rock hard as he watched the sway of her hips and jiggle of her ass in the backless garment. She definitely needs to buy more of these. Vee's legs appeared so long in the Ruthie Davis heels she wore. He would never forget the name of those damn shoes. He'd spent weeks searching everywhere for a specific pair she just had to have. Cornelius had completely forgotten about the chef until he cleared his throat.

"The first course is served."

Cornelius locked eyes with Victoria and neither one of them was thinking about food.

"Stop looking at me like that Cornelius, I'm not on the menu" she said with a raised eyebrow.

"Not yet, Che're, not yet"

She blushed so beautifully. Vee has a very slick mouth. Her quick wit and perfectly timed zingers and puns kept him on his toes. There's never a dull moment with her. The couple managed to finish dinner as well as dessert. He didn't know why she planned such an elaborate dinner and greatly appreciated the thought she put into it. He was ready to ravish her though, wanting her in his arms without that bra immediately. The thought entered his mind to allow Vee to briefly keep on the panties since the flimsy garment wouldn't interfere with his access to her sweetness and those high ass heels, she's wearing are just sexy as fuck.

"Baby..."

"I'll be right back!"

This must be one of those nights when she wanted to be chased by him and pinned down, Cornelius assumed. As he stood up from the table, she returned with one of her hands behind her back.

"Baby, sit down please."

He obliged her since her face was so serious suddenly.

"What's..." She placed one finger over his mouth to silence him. He licked her finger as she traced her hand over his bottom lip. Her sharp intake of breath caused his growing erection to stretch against the zipper in his jeans.

"We've been married for a while and I've tried my best to be the wife you deserve. We have two amazing and handsome boys. You support my dreams. You help me conquer my fears. You spoil us all rotten. I couldn't ask for a better husband. But..."

But?!

"...you deserve a better wife. I haven't been fair to you. I have been holding back and not fully invested in our life together. However, from this day and going forward, I want you to know that I'm all in and I hope that this proves it to you."

A single tear slid down her sweet face and he became distracted by the slight sadness in her eyes that he didn't see her bring her other hand from behind her back.

Victoria

Why isn't he saying anything?

"Cornelius? You don't like it?"

He shifted his gaze to look at the gray box in my hand. Cornelius's eyes shot back up at me and a huge smile spread across his face. The ring, a halo of emerald cut diamonds in a white gold setting is entirely too flashy for his taste, but the plain titanium band that he currently wore spoke volumes when compared to the ring I wear.

"I love everything you do for me, li'l big momma."

I blushed slightly and giggled like a child. He picked me up and I wrapped my legs around his waist. Our lips locked as the moisture began to pool at the apex of my thighs. As he carried me to our bedroom, one of his hands that was firmly cupping my cheek, slid to my lower lips and his fingers penetrated the wetness and heat of my yoni. I love him so much and it's about time I allow myself to be *in* love with him.

Cornelius

He was mesmerized by his wife's beauty. When she first cut her hair off, he was livid beyond explanation. The thrill of running his fingers through her hair, especially when he was deep inside her throat, was a feeling too joyfully complicated for words to explain. However, this short cut gives a new perspective to her features. He loves his wife dearly and even strongly likes the new ring she bought him, even though it's not his style at all. He decided to leave her sleeping and go take a shower. As inconvenient as it is going to be, Cornelius decided to call AT&T to change his cell number. Although he had already blocked Tiffany, she still called from anonymous numbers which led him to believe she's going to be a problem as long as she has access to him.

Chapter

Ten

"Tracey, you can't be serious right now." I started rubbing my forehead.

"I'm sorry but I can't take you today. I can squeeze you in tomorrow..."

"I've had a standing appointment every Friday morning for over a year and all of a sudden you don't remember my appointment? Okay, that's fine."

I turned and walked away to leave. I had been Tracey's

client since she was fresh out of high school with her cosmetology license. I'd never considered her to be an elite hair stylist, but her prices were reasonable, and she listened to instructions in regard to how I wanted my hair styled, but ever since Colin's funeral, she's been acting strange. It's awful that it took the death of my son for me to re-evaluate the circle of people I surrounded myself with. First, it was my former fiancé' Eric, then my ex-best friend Meka and now my deceased child's godmother was looking to be added to the list. As I neared the entrance to the salon, I realized that Fred, another stylist who worked in the salon was working that day and so I stopped by his station.

"Hey Fred! Are you super busy today?"

"Hey gorgeous! Nah, honey I'm not busy. What's up?"

I explained to him what just happened with Tracey and Fred gladly slayed my hair. I'm sure it was only because we'd formed an acquaintanceship due to my regular visits. As I was hugging Fred to leave, Tracey came over to make her catty comments.

"Thank you for taking care of my client Fred".

I just looked at her and rolled my eyes.

"See you next week Fred... Bye Tracey".

****

There's an old saying that if you're not in a storm, you're either just leaving one or about to enter one. In my case, I was about to enter the biggest storm of my life. It started with my husband changing his cell number. I've always been an attentive person. Attention to details is paramount to me, so when my husband changed his cell number...

I noticed.

When my husband's visits to his hometown of Slidell increased...

I noticed.

I called Dodie; she always had the best advice. I know she would help me look at the entire situation of my marriage and keep me from flipping out and falsely accusing my husband of something. I may be biased but, my mommy is the best mother in the universe. The older I became and since becoming a mother again, my admiration for her grew tremendously. Biologically Dodie is my maternal grandmother. When I was about 3 months old, she began to keep me pretty regularly. Lynn, her daughter wasn't making the best decisions at that time in her life. So, before CPS removed me from Lynn's custody as they had with my older brother, Dodie stepped in to keep me in the family. It wasn't an easy transition to go from granddaughter to daughter for my family members. My uncle and aunts became my brother and sisters, and my cousins became my nieces and nephews. Over the years, everyone came to terms with it. Almost everyone anyway. Lynn, for some reason chose to take the victim mentality. She would tell anyone who would listen that Dodie stole me from her. As a child, I fell into her web of manipulation by believing her lies. Once I became a mother, her lies made no sense and at that point I realized her true intentions, which was to drive a wedge between Dodie and myself.

Since Cornelius was out of town, I decided to take the kids to my parents' house for some quality time. The boys loved their grandparents. I think very highly of my parent's marriage. My dad is my mom's second husband. Dodie's first marriage only ended with the death of her first husband. That's a rare quality these days. She's been married to my dad for 30 years. I didn't bother to retrieve my keys to their house since I was carrying Christian and holding onto Cade's hand tightly. I rang the doorbell repeatedly; nobody came to the door. I begrudgingly put Christian down to dig through my bag to find the key. After I opened the door, I noticed that the lights were on.

"Momma!"

No answer.

I checked the garage, and her truck was there.

"Momma!"

No answer.

I checked the backyard and my dad's truck wasn't there so maybe they were together and would return soon.

I went to use the restroom. The door wouldn't open. This is odd. The door seemed to be stuck.

I picked up my cell phone to call my mommy. Her phone began to resound from the desk in her office. An unusual feeling began to creep over me. Dodie never left the house without her phone. I disconnected the call and turned my attention back to the bathroom door. After several attempts, I finally shoved the door with all the might I had and was able to create a small crack to see through.

"Momma!!" I shrieked.

My eyes had to be playing tricks on me. My brain was already beginning to deny what my sight was registering. A low small voice reached my ears "What's wrong mommy?"

"Cade go back into the other room with Christian!"

I didn't mean to yell at my son; however, panic had already enveloped me. Finally, with everything I had in me, I was able to get the door opened. I had no choice but to acknowledge what was keeping the door from opening. On the floor, lay the lifeless body of my dearly beloved mother. I didn't think it was possible to experience this level of pain more than once in a lifetime. I was wrong... so very, very wrong.

Chapter

Eleven

I snatched my phone and called 911. After I hung up the phone, I dropped to my knees next to my mommy. I could tell that she hadn't been there long. There was still perspiration on her forehead. I grabbed a towel and wiped the sweat from her brow. I knew that I shouldn't, but I moved my mother over slightly so that I could clean up the mess. While a part of me acknowledged that she wasn't alive, the part of me that would forever be her "little one" couldn't allow the responding officers to see her in that condition. As

I cleaned her off, I felt ashamed when I saw her toes. She was overdue for a pedicure and I had been putting it off. It's a minor detail but in those moments, the long list of "could've... would've... should've" plays out in your head. As I finished the task of cleaning my mother, the first responders rang the doorbell. I gently kissed my mommy on her forehead and whispered, "I love you, mommy."

Once, I opened the door everything spiraled into a blur after that. My father and brother arrived shortly before the ambulance left. On the way to the hospital, I called my sisters and Stacie to give them the news. By the time Dodie was taken into surgery, everyone had arrived at Memorial Herman in the medical center. Once my dad walked in with my boys, I went outside to get some air. Even the outdoors seemed to be closing in on me. Thankfully, the boys were quiet which allowed me to breathe through the oncoming anxiety attack I was experiencing. My phone rang.

"Hey! I'm in the ER, where are you?"

"I'm outside the ambulance entrance sitting on the curb."

"Ok, here I come".

Stacie is the sister that I've always needed. Stacie taught me that family isn't always the people that you share DNA with.

She walked up and gently took Christian from my arms. I took the opportunity to call my husband.

"The caller you are trying to reach is unavailable..."

That was the fourth call. Cornelius has never not answered my calls. Lately, he's been answering less and less. It doesn't take a rocket scientist to figure out that we definitely have a disconnect in our marriage.

"Stacie, I've called him 4 times and he's still not answering."

"Maybe he's sleeping or..."

"I've never called him this many times back-to-back. Ever. He's been acting differently for some months now. I thought we were in a better space."

"I think you should just be patient and don't jump to conclusions. You're in a really sensitive place right now. Look, I'm going to take the boys with me, and you can pick them up tomorrow. Focus on momma right now and call me when the doctors are done with surgery."

"Thanks, Stace... I'll call you later."

I kissed the boys and watched them walk into the building. As the sun was setting, my phone finally rang.

"Hello"

It was Cornelius.

"Hey my love"

My eyes rolled towards the sky.

"Where are you?"

"I'm on I-10 now, just passed through Lafayette."

My sister came running up to me, "Come on, the doctor's want to meet with us now!"

"Cornelius, I have to go. Dodie is in the hospital. I'll call you later."

"Baby, wha-"

I disconnected the call. We both ran inside the building.

Eric

He could see the minister's lips moving but there was no voice to be heard. He looked around and saw Ray looking back at him. He nodded his head and Eric nodded back and then turned to look at the woman next to him. Victoria looked absolutely gorgeous. He leaned in to kiss her. It was a simple kiss that ignited so much passion. He grabbed the sides of her face and held her there. When he felt his manhood awaken, he released her. Eric opened his intoxicated eyes and blinked hard. The eyes that he was now looking into were not almond shaped but round instead and the face that beamed was not caramel complected but a rich chocolate. In his drunken haze, Eric reminded himself that it was Monica he was in Vegas eloping with. Not Victoria. What had he done...?

Eric felt like a sledgehammer was being slammed against his head rhythmically. He tried to sit up and everything started to spiral in a blurry haze. The last time he had been this drunk and hungover was right after Colin died. He never had properly grieved for his only son. All those pent-up emotions were released onto Colin's mother which was the catalyst for the destruction of their relationship. Now they were both married to people that weren't who their hearts wanted. Well at least that was the case for Eric. Victoria gave the impression that she was deliriously happy. He had not spoken with her since their last meeting at the Aquarium. Vee had blocked his number, stopped talking to his sister and seemingly cut all ties to him. None of their mutual friends had seen her and she deleted her Twitter. He thought about his wife, Monica was safe. She didn't challenge him the way Victoria did. Monica was completely absorbed with her son and now her marriage. Victoria was like a bonfire, gives the appearance of being containable but realistically can't be. Why didn't see just say what he needed her to say? Why did she leave without a word? All Eric needed was a reaction from Victoria. Her stubbornness irritated the hell out of him, but... but they were done and now they both have to deal with the decisions they've made. Eric knew he would find a way to get her back in his life. He had to. Wife or no wife, Victoria is his life and he refused to live without her. Eric would never embarrass Monica, but...

388 | P a g e

Cornelius

He had to call five different people until someone finally answered to give him the information he needed. His mother-in-law was in the hospital. She suffered a stroke caused by an aneurysm. Victoria was staying at the hospital overnight which meant she wouldn't be home until the next morning. If she even came home at all. She'd probably go stay at her parents' house since that was much closer to the hospital. Cornelius knew that Victoria was probably livid with him but knowing her as well as he did, he knew she would push their issues to the back burner until the situation with her mother was resolved. He'd been working extra hard in his hometown closing his businesses and ensuring a smooth transition for his former employees into new positions with other companies. Unbeknownst to his wife, he'd also been transferring his responsibilities with his drug connection onto his best friend. Neither party was elated that he was retiring completely. He had to, otherwise, as he suspected, he would lose his family. Vee hadn't said anything directly but things between them had definitely changed for the worst. His phone rang.

"Hey, just a heads up, I'm not coming home, and the boys are with Stace".

"That's cool baby. Have you eaten? Do you need anything?"

"I called you four times."

The depth of tiredness that emanated from her voice bothered Cornelius deeply.

"I called you back as soon as I saw your missed calls."

"Ok"

He definitely knew what her ok meant. She was starting to close off. He had to fix that quickly.

"Love, is your car there or will you need a ride home?"

"I'll catch a cab to my parent's house, once my sister arrives in the morning."

"Which one and what time is she coming?"

"Nadine. She'll be here before the shift change at 6a."

"Ok baby, get some rest if you can. Kiss momma for me and I'll see you tomorrow."

The call disconnected. Victoria didn't say bye nor "I love you"... she's angry.

Victoria

When I found my mother on that white tiled bathroom floor, I thought she was already gone. However, the paramedics were able to find a pulse. It was barely there. My momma was a fighter, which is where I get that same energy from. Her strength was amazing. The doctor said the surgery was successful, but she went into a coma shortly after and they called my father, my siblings and myself into a meeting to give us a status update as a group since a "decision had to be made". Those words sent a cold chill down my spine. The last time I was told those words, I had to sign paperwork to let go of my son. We entered a huge meeting room and as the doctor was explaining all the various outcomes that could take place, in walked Lynn. I hadn't seen this woman in years. At the very moment all my anger and disgust surged over me like a tidal wave. I returned my attention to the doctor.

"So, in essence, Mrs. Gafford will be in a vegetative state indefinitely. We've done all that we can. We will give you some time to discuss your options and when you make a decision just have the nurse to page me."

As soon as the door closed behind the doctor. The proverbial shit hit the fan.

Momma wouldn't want this...

Who's going to take care of her?...

I don't have the space...

The excuses started to spread like a wildfire. None of which mattered to me since, I will gladly move my mommy into my home with me, vegetative state or not. However, I'd already been down this road...

"We need to just pull the plug and let momma be free, she wouldn't..."

Lynn had the audacity to open her mouth and before I could even register what was happening...

"Bitch, momma didn't even like you so you can keep your unrequested opinions to yourself. You're only here out of courtesy of your other siblings so I suggest you shut the entire fuck up and be as invisible as possible."

"I will be-"

"You'll be buried right next to momma if you say another word."

The room was deathly silent.

As I surveyed, the faces in the room I was consumed with rage and utter disgust. My mother had co-signed for homes and cars for many of the people in this room not including myself, yet I was the only one who wanted to fight for her. I took that opportunity to educate everyone that while they may have opinions, my mother was married to *my* father, their stepfather and ultimately it was *his* decision and in case no one noticed, he was zoned out which meant my daddy would only be listening to me, his *only* daughter. After I said my peace, I grabbed my daddy's hand, and we exited the room.

****

My eyes were bloodshot red, dry, and as heavy as the bags underneath my eyes. My favorite pair of darkly tinted Dolce & Gabbana shades hid my weary gaze. I held tightly to the hand grasped firmly in mine - the walk to the front of the church seemed to be 1000 miles long - praying that my knees wouldn't give out. I had survived the death of my son, a vicious sexual assault, and a criminal trial that could have landed me behind bars for years to life and now this... I refuse to shed a tear. Those would come soon enough. Instead, I boldly let go of the hand that held mine, courageously approached the casket. There lay Dodie, still as beautiful as ever - she looks so peaceful. This was the woman that had raised me, nurtured me, loved me, taught me all she knew about life, stood by my side through trials and tribulations, joyous occasions, thick and thin. Most importantly, she'd introduced me to her greatest friend of all: Jesus Christ.

"Mommy, thank you for everything. I'm going to miss you, and I will always love you," I whispered. Gently leaning in, I kissed my mother on the forehead one final time, and then took my seat.

As the funeral director lowered the lid on my mother's casket, I began to play Dodie's favorite song, "What a Friend We Have in Jesus."

After everything I've been through, as much as it hurt like hell, there was absolutely no doubt that I would, like a mythical phoenix, rise from these flames, as resilient as ever. After I played the ending notes, I stood up from the piano seat and slowly walked back to the pew to join my father on the front row. As I took my seat, I glanced across the aisle towards my husband. That title caused me to cringe. I wouldn't give any energy to my issues with him today. I wish he weren't even here. Unbeknownst to me, he was appointed as a pallbearer. An honor, in my opinion, that he didn't deserve. However, deep inside I was grateful that he wasn't sitting next to me and I could at least get through the service without additional emotional stress.

Cornelius

"I'm filing for divorce."

Victoria's voice was so matter of fact; it almost didn't register that she was talking to him. Cornelius walked out of the closet still in the process of removing his necktie.

"You're doing what?"

"I'm filing for divorce. I'm done"

Laughter escaped him and the look on Victoria's face caused him to laugh harder... until awareness grasped him.

"For what?! There's no reason to go to that extreme. Just beca..."

Victoria stared at *her* husband blankly.

"Who is Tiffany."

It was more of a statement than a question, but it caused Cornelius to freeze. It seemed as if time stopped completely as they stood staring into each other's eyes. He didn't know how long it took to register but he finally saw the rage that was in his wife's eyes.

Victoria

This stupid muthafucker just standing here looking caught. He's like a deer caught in 18-wheeler headlights. To be honest, I'm not even angry. Well not about his cheating anyway. The part that angers me is how the man who claimed to love me so much couldn't or wouldn't even at least postpone his cheating to allow me to grieve for my mother in peace. He still hasn't said a word.

"Look, I'll make this simple. I'll get the paperwork drawn up and I'll contact you when I need your signature. As long as you don't attempt to dispute the divorce then I won't request child support. We both can move on peacefully with our lives."

" I'm not giving up on our marriage. I lo-"

"Yeah, I'm not listening, and I'll be moving out. I'll send a company to pack up my stuff."

With that said, I turned to leave. I went into the boys' room and packed a bag for them. As we were walking out the front door Bones decided to plead a final time.

" Baby, please don't take my kids. Don't leave like this!"

"Dude... you have other children, go play with them. Save your begging for Tiffany."

I put on my seatbelt, started my truck, and left.

****

I was running as fast as my legs would move. I couldn't see what was chasing me or rather what I was running from. The darkness was suffocating... My eyes jerked open... I'm not dreaming...I can't breathe! I clawed at my neck and in my panic, I fell to the floor.

"Mommy!"

In the dim moonlight, my eyes fixated on the two sets of eyes staring back at me full of fear. Then the darkness consumed us all.

I've replayed my death over and over in my mind more than once. None of those scenarios involved an excruciating headache. So obviously I'm not dead. I slowly opened one eye then the other and surveyed my surroundings. My daddy was seated in the chair with Cade laying on his chest, in the corner of the room. My brother half on and half hanging off of the mini sofa with Christian laying on his chest, by the wall. I'm in a hospital bed. I have no idea which one or why. I pushed the red button on the remote to call the nurse. After a few minutes she entered quietly with a beaming smile on her face.

"Good Morning, Mrs. Arceneaux how are you feeling?"

" I feel slightly weak, what happened to me and where am I?"

"You're at the Woman's Hospital of Texas. Your gall bladder ruptured, and you were immediately sent into surgery. Thankfully no significant damage was done, and everything is fine and so is your baby."

"Baby? What baby?"

Even as I finished asking the question, my mind began racing to recall my last monthly cycle. I couldn't.

"You weren't aware of your pregnancy?"

"No"

The immediate sadness that gripped me sent the monitors attached to me into an uproar. The nurse instructed me to lay back and breathe deeply. She then pushed a button on the device keypad and almost instantly I drifted back off into a deep sleep.

I awoke later that afternoon to an empty room. I reached for my phone on the bedside table and called Stacie. The tears started as soon as she answered the phone.

"I'm pregnant"

"Who is this?!"

"It's me, Vee!"

"What's wrong? You don't even sound like yourself?"

"I'm at the hospital..."

I brought her up to date on what had transpired overnight and my current state. How could I be pregnant? My husband and I hadn't been intimate in months. Between his deceptions and my mother's death, I didn't have the energy. I was trying to keep myself from imploding mentally. My boys were the only stability in my life. They depended on me to be as stable as I could for them. After I ended the call with Stacie, I searched the calendar on my iPhone for some type of indication of how far along I could be. There was no record of a monthly cycle nor a sexual contact for almost 6 1/2 months. There's no way that could be right, could it? I decided I would deal with that after I was released from the hospital. My phone rang again this time I rolled my eyes so hard they almost got stuck.

"What do you want, Bones?"

"Oh? I'm Bon... whatever."

He released a defeated sigh.

"I'm just calling to check on you. You are still my wife and the mother of my children."

I hung up in his face. I felt the urge to vomit and lurched over the side of the bed into the small trash can. My aim was not successful. Some of the mess splashed onto the floor. The beeping resumed on the machine alerting the attending nurse that my blood pressure had elevated once again. Nurse Wooten, rubbed my back until I finished and then methodically cleaned up the mess, checked the bed to ensure that the sheets wouldn't need to be changed, cleaned my face with a cool, damp towel and then brought me ice chips.

Hospitals have the best ice for chewing. Pregnant women have the strangest observations. My next observation is I'm 29, grieving daughter, pregnant, mother of two toddlers and planning a divorce. The tears flowed like a river down my face and mommy was no longer here to make it better and console me. The hollow space inside grew and I can feel the emptiness.

Cornelius

He looked around the room as if the cream-colored walls would give him the answers to his questions or a solution to what was about to become a detrimental problem. His wife was barely speaking to him outside of her nonsense about getting the divorce. Cornelius had to resort to seeming to be cooperative just to hear her voice regularly. When he wanted to see the boys, she demanded he text her. The shit was ridiculous, however he indulged it because he knew that if he gave her some space she would eventually calm down, forgive him, and bring her ass home. He cut Tiffany off without an explanation. Even though he gave Tiffany the ammunition against him, he still couldn't understand why she felt the need to tell his wife about the affair. As if that would change her status in his life. Tiffany blew up his phone day and night with calls and texts. He ignored it all. He was focused on stopping this divorce and getting his life back on track. Victoria and their kids are his world. She was the only woman that loved his older kids as her own. It wasn't forced at all. Cornelius was so deep in thought; he hadn't heard the doctor even re-enter the room.

"Ok, Mr. Arceneaux we'll send your prescription over to the clinic and just take the medicine as prescribed and everything will clear up in 7 days. Please refrain from any and all sexual contact during that time. If you have any questions, call the office. Good luck to you sir." Fed up with being ignored, Tiffany finally called him from another phone number and when he answered she gave him the final nail to the coffin his marriage was in...

"You gave me chlamydia and I'm pregnant, congratulations."

Before he could respond, Tiffany hung up the phone. He tried calling back repeatedly. He wanted badly to cuss her out, but she wouldn't answer and whoever the phone belongs to had blocked him since at one point the calls started going straight to voice mail. He wanted to believe it was a sick joke just to get his attention, however he knew deep inside that even if she was joking, one of her statements had to be true. Unfortunately for him, it turned out to be both.

Cornelius attempted to call Victoria repeatedly to no avail. So, he decided to show up unannounced at her parent's home.

Victoria

I had experienced so much in my life that when my own red flags started to wave, I noticed. I was so lost in thought that I never heard the chants from the irate crowd as I exited the building.

"Murderer!!"

"A fetus is a life!"

Instantly, I gathered myself and glanced around to see that a protest group was gathered outside of the abortion clinic I was leaving.

"I didn't even get an abortion, get your dumb ass out of my face!"

I was livid. Until today, I personally had not believed in abortion either. However, I wasn't judgmental enough to protest what other women do with their own bodies. I feel so lost, like I don't know what to do. To make matters worse, my mommy was no longer alive to help me through this. I got into my truck and started driving aimlessly, until I found myself on 290. I called the one person I could that I know wouldn't judge and would definitely help me process my current state of events.

After crying myself breathless, in between breathing heaves...

"I'm pregnant"

Maurice stood up from his seat and sat next to me. Placed his arm around my shoulder and just hugged me. Once my breathing normalized, I began to explain.

"I just left the abortion clinic. I had no idea..." The sobs began again. Abortions are a two-day process. The first day you come in you fill out paperwork, take a pregnancy test, watch a video on the pros and cons and also alternative options. The second day, because of new state law regulations, women now have to look at a sonogram of the fetus before the actual procedure is done. My experience stopped at the sonogram. Once the nurse placed the nodule onto my tummy, the look of dread that crossed her face scared me instantly.

"Mrs. Arceneaux, we won't be able to proceed with the procedure."

"What? why??"

"This is against company policy, but..."

When she turned the screen around, my mouth dropped. I'd given birth enough times to know that I had to be about 6 1/2 to 7 months pregnant.

Cornelius

He pressed the doorbell twice.

He waited.

A shadow passed the peephole.

"What the fuck do you want."

The anger in her voice burned him.

"Please open the door, Victoria."

His voice was nervously calm.

Two minutes passed.

He heard the locks turning.

The door was snatched open.

"What. In. The. Fuck. Do. You. Want."

"Can I come... Will you come outside?"

Her eyes held a murderous gaze. Maybe the door should've remained between them.

"There's no easy way to say this. Vee, you need to go to the doctor..."

Her countenance changed and confusion covered her.

"Why do I need to go to the doctor?"

"I have chlamydia and I..."

His vision was blurred, and the floating dots of light signified that he hadn't died. The ringing in his ear and the throbbing sting in his face, aligned with the way Victoria was shaking her hand vigorously indicated that she had indeed slapped him with all the strength she could muster.

He stumbled backwards and his face felt as if it were on fire. He knew she would be angry. He expected it. Cornelius did not expect to be slapped. It was a befitting response that he hadn't anticipated.

"You low-life dirty dick... you know what, you're not even worth my anger. I don't have anything your stupid ass has, you dumb son of a bitch. We haven't had sex in 7 months. If your nasty ass wasn't so self-absorbed with your cheating, then you would know that. Your sorry ass begged me to marry you! You begged me to give you a chance! Begged me to have your babies and this is what I get in return? A narcissistic, toxic, selfish asshole. Well guess what? I'm pregnant again, dumb ass and *We* are STD free. My only regret is that I'm too far into it to get an abortion!"

"Wa-"

"Get the fuck off my property and stay the fuck away from me!"

Victoria turned around, walked into the house and out of his life.

Victoria

"It's my birthday! Why must everything be about this baby?"

Stacie rolled her eyes. It was another one of my tantrums that she ignored. She was happy to be an "aunt" again especially since this time, I'm having a girl. Stacie brushed off my rants and indifference as hormonal but deep inside, I wasn't happy at all. I was in the middle of a very nasty divorce. Cornelius was fighting me every step of the way. All of a sudden, he wanted half of everything except custody of the kids. I found out about Tiffany's pregnancy. I destroyed our home and removed every trace of me and the kids from it, then it put it up for sale. I would typically be all excited and super happy about being pregnant. This time, even when the baby would kick, I rolled my eyes. Maurice called regularly to check on me. Sometimes we would talk and sometimes I would ignore his calls and text messages. After the last time I saw Cornelius, my doctor confirmed that I was 7 months exactly. Between losing my mother, Cornelius's infidelities and trying to keep my businesses operational, I hadn't noticed that I missed monthly cycles and attributed the weight gain to my tumultuous life. Now it was my 30th birthday and instead of being focused on me, my best friend was throwing me a baby shower as a gift. I was not amused and was slightly ungrateful.

"You're being very petty by not picking out a name. Any other time you'd have a name picked out by now."

She was right. I would. This time was different. I was angry and utterly terrified. My mommy wasn't going to be there to hold my hand. How was I going to get through this?

"Princess C looks tacky on this cake."

Stacie was not letting up. She must be really tired of my mood swings. I laughed. She did have a valid point though.

"Princess C" did look weird. I inwardly chastised myself.

"Ok, fine... I'll have a name by the time she gets here."

****

Two months later, I didn't even have time to worry about who was going to hold my hand while I gave birth. The boys and I were out shopping when my water broke. I had to drive myself to the hospital. As soon as I changed into the hospital gown and the monitors were placed on my stomach, my contractions were on coming in non-stop waves. As Stacie came rushing into the room, I was unintentionally bearing down and the nurse was hurriedly calling for the doctor and staff, I was curled into a ball watching a small hairy ball emerge from between my legs. The nurse yelled for me to stop pushing however, I had no control over what was going on. As the doctor rushed in, I had locked eyes with the small invader who was forcing her way out into the world. A tear slid down my face at the thought that I almost didn't have this experience because I tried to abort her. The guilt was overwhelming. Seconds later, she Cassidy Victoria was laying on my chest. She didn't cry like her brothers had, she just opened her eyes and looked at me. All my resentment, anger and guilt melted away and I thanked God for blessing me with her in spite of my horrible decisions. A warm feeling of completion came over me. I felt whole.

****

Windsong Resort, Turks, and Caicos, 8 months later

As I began to read the email from my attorney, I glanced up at Cade and Christian building their sandcastle and Cassidy was still sleeping. This website didn't do this place any justice at all. The sand is almost white, and the water is a beautiful indigo blue.

I have great news for you! Everything has been finalized, the judge signed off on the divorce paperwork today. You can pick up your copies once you return to the states. The proceeds for your home and salon sales are scheduled for deposit in three days. Congratulations, Ms. Gafford, enjoy your vacation and I'll see you when you return.

I powered off my iPhone and laid back on the chaise.

"What are you smiling about?"

"Girl... it's finally over! Everything is complete and Cornelius is finally out of my life."

Stacie broke out into a faux praise dance and we both laughed heartily. I picked up my pineapple with the purple umbrella in it, I was done breast feeding and we were on a beautiful island for the next 7 days. A few hours after I gave birth to Cassidy, there was a knock on my door. In walked Eric, with a bouquet of flowers and balloons. We talked and it was nice to talk to someone who'd been there before life had happened to me. We promised to remain friends ... real friends this time. I'm optimistic about it. Right now, I'm just thankful to God that I have Stacie and the kids to enjoy this country with. I have no idea what's next in life, but I do know that what my mommy would say all the time is comforting.

"I don't know what tomorrow holds, but I do know *WHO* holds tomorrow and *HE* holds my hand."

Chapter Thirteen

"It was all good just a week ago" I thought to myself as I watched the meteorologist on the news station give his predictions on the forecast for Hurricane Harvey. Two weeks ago, my oldest son, Cade became a teenager, and we celebrated his birthday with a Hip Hop/Rap costume party. Cade went dressed as Tupac, our favorite rapper. Christian was dressed as Snoop D oh double G leaving Cassidy and myself as Salt -n- Peppa.

"Cade! Christian! Cassidy! Rise and shine, it's time to get ready for school."

I turned off the alarm and slid into my robe. As I neared their bedrooms, the children filed out of the rooms and into their respective restrooms to brush their teeth and wash their faces.

"Good morning my loves!" I said with such glee which was returned with mumbled and dry responses. I finally came to terms with the fact that my children just were not morning people, after sending them to bed at an earlier time didn't change their demeanor in the mornings.

"Mommy I don't wanna go to school today."

"Cassidy, you never want to go to school any day."

I laughed it off and shooed her away to finish getting dressed. The familiar ping from my iPhone alerted me to a new email. With a roll of my eyes, I opened my virtual mailbox hoping that whatever the message was, wouldn't ruin my day. Even though my divorce was finalized, I still found myself in family court every few months because Cornelius decided that since he couldn't have me anymore, he wouldn't take care of his children. The back and forth was getting really old really quickly. Sure enough, it was an email from my attorney with the latest updates from the deadbeat's legal shenanigans.

To: Victoria Gafford

From: Roy Jenkins

Good Morning,

I just wanted to give you an update on the present standings of your case. We filed a motion to have the child support terminated, although I strongly advised against that. I have since received copies of the motions filed by the defendant. He is now requesting DNA testing on all the children. This is merely a stall tactic as all three children were born inside of the marriage, Mr. Arceneaux has no grounds to stand on. The judge will more than likely throw that out.

Now, in regard to the other matter you inquired about...

I believe it would be best to schedule an in-person meeting to discuss all the intricate details. Contact my secretary and schedule a conference at your earliest convenience.

Don't be upset, this is just another step in an unfortunately lengthy process, however there is an end and hopefully a successful one for us.

Best Regards,

Roy Jenkins, Esq.

I was trying my best not to allow my anger to overtake me. It was a challenge. I can't believe the audacity!

Cornelius was definitely taking this to a new low. I honestly don't even know why I'm surprised. I rolled my eyes, dropped the phone in my purse and hustled the kids to the SUV. My day wasn't going to be derailed by a deadbeat's antics. I gathered my children and rushed them into my truck so that I wouldn't add being late to school to the list of what could go wrong today.

Stacie

What the fuck am I doing here? Has my life really come to this?

"Yeah, so I just decided to get my auction license and just sell cars..."

Clearly, she missed some information by being lost in her own thoughts because what the *gentleman*, and she used *that* term loosely, said wasn't making sense.

"Wait, you live in an apartment, correct?

"Yeah"

"And you keep the cars you're selling in the parking lot of your complex?"

"Yeah"

Stacie stared blankly for a few seconds and then shook her head as if trying to fling off the utter disbelief she was experiencing. She picked up her clutch and got up from the table.

"Thank you for inviting me out but this clearly isn't going to work."

"Huh? You're leaving? The food hasn't been brought to the table. I'm not paying for food you not gonna eat! What the fuck kinda silly shit are you on?"

His grammar made her cringe inwardly and his volume drew a few glances. After quickly surveying their surroundings, she realized that she definitely had no business being here with this guy. Stacie rolled her eyes and with all the calmness she could muster reached into her clutch and pulled out a crisp bill and placed it on the table.

"This is the best $100 I've ever spent."

She then turned and strutted out of the restaurant that she was completely over dressed to be in.

"This place doesn't even have valet." She thought to herself.

Stacie decided in that moment she was taking a break from dating. Either the pool had gotten extremely shallow, or she had finally reached rock bottom, either way, a break was desperately needed. After she was safely tucked away in her AMG S 63, she tapped a button on the steering wheel and after 3 rings, a hushed voice answered the call.

"Hey, did I wake you or the kids?"

"No, I wasn't asleep, and the kids are knocked out. How was the date?"

"Girl!! It was horrible! I left before the food even arrived."

Stacie spent the entire journey home, sharing the details of this failed excursion to her best friend Vee. They were both laughing hysterically by the time Stacie arrived at the entrance to her gated community.

Stacie lived in the Blevins Estates, a posh subdivision in Cypress, Texas. It was her dream home. She had worked hard all her life to achieve what she had. The only thing missing was a "mister".

"He did WHAT?!"

Stacie couldn't believe what Vee had just told her.

"Yes, ma'am… that sorry sack of shit is now asking the court for DNA testing. This is why I told Roy to just have all of it terminated. I don't have the energy for this. No one should have to go through this for a person to take care of their children."

Stacie had to agree, no one should have to go through all of this just to take care of their children. However, she didn't agree with Vee on terminating the court order.

"Even though he isn't paying anything Vee, you should still keep the order in place. That way, no matter what happens, if he comes into a lot of money or if he decides to grow up, you'll have everything in place already.

Vee pondered what her friend was saying, and as usual Stacie made a valid point.

"So when are you and your future husband going on a second date?" Vee began to laugh so hard that tears formed in her eyes.

"Girl, go to hell!" Stacie hung up on Vee who was still laughing.

EPILOGUE

After a lengthy legal battle, Victoria was triumphant in her case against Cornelius. Due to his verbal abuse towards their oldest son, his visitation was limited to supervised visits one hour, once a week. Eventually Cornelius stopped showing up and after three missed visits, Vee stopped as well. The children began counseling and with a little time and lots of love, Vee was able to get them on the path to mental and emotional stability.

Vee and Eric became best friends again. After all the heart ache they've both experienced and the losses that life has dealt them, they realized that the love they have for one another was too valuable to allow it to dissipate. While they have no intentions of a romantic nature towards each other, who knows what the future holds?

Afterword

I want to start by first and foremost, thanking you for purchasing and reading my book. I'm truly and eternally grateful. I'm listening to "My Testimony" by Marvin Sapp. It's a beautiful and very fitting song to my life. This process for me has been remarkably similar, in theory, to being pregnant and giving birth. Needless to say, I am one proud momma! I want to bring attention to Suicide Awareness. We, as a society get so wrapped up in our own stuff that we miss the warning signs and red flags. Being on both sides of that particular subject, I know that yes, people can hide. I hid my contemplation and attempt at suicide very well, however I also know that because my mommy and my best friend took the time to be observant and give a little extra attention, through God I was saved and I'm still here to share my experiences with you. While majority of this novel is fiction, some of the events did actually happen. My goal... my purpose... is to show every person who reads this book or even discusses this book that you can overcome anything. No matter how challenging the situation may be, you can still come out on top. Life is a roller coaster ride; hold on throughout the lows to enjoy all the highs! Pay attention to the people you love. If you see something, then say something. A simple smile can make a huge difference in a person's life. A smile may save a life.

Blessing...Love...Light

- VS Griffin